SOUL PURSUIT

A JACK STERLING DETECTIVE NOVEL

CHIP TUDOR

SOUL PURSUIT
Copyright © 2019 Chip Tudor

All rights reserved. No part of this publication may be reproduced, distributed, or transmitted in any form or by any means, including photocopying, recording, or other electronic or mechanical methods, without the prior written permission of the publisher, except in the case of brief quotations embodied in critical reviews and certain other noncommercial uses permitted by copyright law.

References to historical events, real people, or real places are used fictitiously.

Cover Design by James Graves.

Published by Chip Tudor Communications, Inc. in the United States of America.

Publisher's Cataloging-in-Publication Data provided by Five Rainbows Cataloging Services

Names: Tudor, Chip, author.
Title: Soul pursuit : a Jack Sterling detective novel / Chip Tudor.
Description: Dayton, OH : Chip Tudor Communications, 2019. | Also available in ebook and audiobook formats.
Identifiers: ISBN 978-1-0919-8348-9 (paperback)
Subjects: LCSH: United States. Navy. SEALs--Fiction. | Bounty hunters--Fiction. | Veterans--Fiction. | Detective and mystery stories. | Christian fiction. | BISAC: FICTION / Christian / Contemporary. | FICTION / Christian / Suspense. | FICTION / Mystery & Detective / General. | GSAFD: Christian fiction. | Mystery fiction.
Classification: LCC PS3620.U36 S68 2019 (print) LCC PS3620.U36 (ebook) | DDC 813/.6--dc23.

~ONE~

I stood on the front porch of a relatively new, relatively large, and relatively expensive home in Centerville, a relatively upper class, south suburban neighborhood of Dayton, Ohio. A friendly reminder that much in life is relative.

A May sun was shining and felt warm on my back. The front yard had been recently and carefully mowed with the musky scent of freshly cut grass thick in the air. I slid a duffle bag strap off my shoulder and let the bag plop at my feet. Then pushed the doorbell and listened to it chime inside.

I was wearing a coat and tie—outside my normal practice and comfort zone. But I tried to hide it from my face. Not sure my face was cooperating. I was eight the last time I wore a coat and tie. Didn't like it then. Didn't now.

Funny how some memories in life disappear into oblivion, some recede into subconsciousness and resurface later at random moments and others are imprinted forever in your mind. There was nothing particularly significant about this one, but it was fresh like yesterday.

I was eight or nine and it was an Easter Sunday when Mom insisted we attend church together as a family. My father reluctantly agreed so we all dressed up in outfits Mom carefully laid out for us and off we went—Dad, Mom, my brother, sister and me.

My dad, brother and I fidgeted uncomfortably in our coats and ties. It's the only memory I have of relating to my father. People at church had pasty smiles on their faces and I wondered if everyone was as happy as they looked on the outside or if church was where you faked happiness regardless of how you actually felt inside. I wasn't happy about it and didn't care if it showed. Don't think Dad was thrilled either, but he managed a friendly smile of sorts.

So my first impression of religion was that it didn't relate much to the rest of life. I enjoyed the jelly beans and marshmallow Easter bunny Mom put in baskets with fake green grass for all of us. And remembered the relief of changing out of the church clothes later. Dad must have felt the same because we never went to church again. But he drilled in other things with military precision. One, whatever is worth doing is worth doing right. And always put your best foot forward.

So, here I stood wearing khaki pants, a navy blue sport coat, and yellow tie bought at a second hand clothes store. Yellow being the power color and all. I tried to look comfortable, at ease and confident. You're supposed to look that way when you wear a power tie.

My face betrayed me though, because the girl, around 12, who opened the front door smothered an immediate smile. Tall and spindly with large brown eyes that presented the candid innocence of a child and the savvy intelligence of a young woman. She studied me a moment. Mentally sorting and classifying. I waited...studying her back.

"You look like a fish out of water," she said.

"SEAL out of water," I said. "Jack Sterling. Have an appointment with Glenn Howard."

She moved aside and motioned me into the foyer. It was spacious with ceramic tiled floor and a high ceiling with hanging chandelier. A wooden staircase on the right extended up and connected at the top to an open hallway that ran perpendicular. She turned and called upstairs.

"Grandpa, the SEAL's here!"

A man's voice replied from a room above.

"Show him up, Samantha."

I smiled at her, keeping the charm wattage on a low three since she was young and impressionable. Didn't want to break her heart.

"Anybody ever call you Sammy?"

She smirked. Might have to up the wattage a little. Maybe not as impressionable as I thought.

"So you're a SEAL," she said with a tone of disappointment.

Navy SEALs had a legendary reputation among military Special Forces. With accomplishments that read like folklore, so people always expected us to look like super heroes. Granted, exactly how we considered ourselves, but in reality came in all shapes and sizes. And none of us bullet proof.

"Was. Now a civilian."

"Don't look all that tough to me."

I smiled again, turning up the wattage to six.

"Wanna arm wrestle?"

Another smirk, but this time with the hint of a real smile. My irresistible charm was kicking in. She nodded her head for me to follow and started up the stairs. The shiny, varnished steps had a carpeted runner down the middle and didn't creak as we climbed. The banister had a smooth touch and similar shine that ended in a curl at the bottom. Sun from a skylight bathed the open space adding friendly warmth.

"Real macho of you. Take on an eleven year old girl."

"But a cute eleven year old girl...who could easily pass for twelve."

She rolled her eyes and twisted her smile into one of all out sarcasm.

"Oh, please. I'm not a little kid."

Apparently, early lessons on the journey into adulthood included denial and cynicism. And Samantha was already mastering both.

"Could probably manage an eleven year old boy too," I added.

"An eleven year old girl who is use to smooth talking sailors full of themselves. How would you rate next to a trained, Ninja warrior?"

We walked along the hallway that over looked the foyer. On the wall hung a number of pictures representing snapshots of family history. A wedding photo of a dashing young military officer with his bride. Then various time stamps of the maturing couple with two children—a boy and girl. Progressions from childhood to adulthood to in-law spouses and grandchildren, including a young Samantha.

"That would require an assistant. Maybe a twelve year old girl. Or an eleven year old who looks twelve."

She stopped and put her hands on her hips with a look of annoyance, but was obviously enjoying the exchange.

"Like I would want to be your sidekick."

I shrugged.

"Every hero needs one. Might even give you a cape. And just so you know, I take prisoners with the sheer force of my magnetic personality."

Her smile widened. My charm was in full effect.

"Then you'll need an army of sidekicks to shoo away all the bugs you attract."

I pumped my chest up with mock offense.

"Army? Young lady, I'm in the Navy!"

She stopped next to the opened door of a room and gestured for me to enter.

"Was. Now I'd say you're washed out."

She gave her hair a flirtatious shake as she retreated down the stairs.

"Well then. See if I ever make a muscle for you."

She waved her hand dismissively without looking back.

"I'd need a magnifying glass."

Glenn Howard watched the exchange quietly, standing by the door.

He was four or five inches taller than his granddaughter, considerably thicker and considerably older. Around sixty by my guess. With wavy, grey hair and thick arms and hands. Even without a uniform, there was a sense of ordered authority about him that cried military. According to my dad he had retired a Brigadier General. And even now, he had a presence that commanded respect.

"Smooth with the ladies I see."

"Sir, when they're under 14 or over 60. In between not so much. That one's going to break a lot of hearts."

Glenn smiled warmly. A soft spot with Grandpa.

"Already has. Let's talk."

We went into his office and I sat in a padded chair across from his desk. I handed him my resume and glanced around the room as he reviewed it dutifully. The desk was a conservative, wood grain model from a moderately priced manufacturer of the do-it-yourself assembly variety.

Behind him, a computer table against the outside wall formed his actual working space. It had a desktop PC, telephone and shelf hutch stocked with resource books related to his trade.

Other features were for show. A book case with volumes by Dickens, Hemingway and other literary giants. A couple of floor plants and a coffee table with two chairs.

A large window with a view out back presented a peaceful and serene picture of forestland and a field of grazing horses. He looked up from the resume and cleared his throat.

"Owe your dad my life," he said. "Picked me up, wounded from an ambush in Nam and carried me to base camp. Would have bled to death otherwise."

I nodded.

"Yes, sir."

I'd heard countless stories like it. My father, the distinguished marine veteran and highly decorated war hero who retired full Colonel. A stranger I knew from a collection of honors and stories of others. My own experience as son involved very little personal contact with him most of my life.

"So, you were a Navy SEAL for nearly 10 years. Why'd you leave?"

"Problems assimilating, sir."

He snorted.

"Describes every SEAL I've ever known. Cockiest bunch of guys on earth. But always glad they were on my side. What team were you on?

"Seven."

He raised his eyebrows.

"Wild Bill?"

"Yes, sir."

He nodded slightly.

"Wild Bill had a reputation for being a Maverick. And you couldn't fit in on his team?"

"I couldn't fit in after he left."

He nodded again like it answered a question in his mind. I waited and he looked at the resume again.

"Got a pretty cushy set-up going here. Mostly conduct routine background checks for Wright Patterson Air Force Base. Doesn't require much, pays well, and with my government pension affords a comfortable life. Mostly phone work, interviewing neighbors, employers and references. Not desperate for help, but do get some field work from time to time."

He didn't have to say it. I knew. This was a favor. I swallowed my pride and said nothing. I needed work and there weren't many opportunities in Dayton, Ohio for someone whose entire resume read covert ops. With perhaps the exception of fast food and retail. I'd no doubt look dashing in a snappy blue vest welcoming in-coming shoppers at the entrance of a super retail store.

He sighed and ran a hand through his gray hair.

"There's a bail bond agent named Carlos Fernandez. Frequently needs someone to assist his clients in showing up for court."

"Assist?"

"The commercial side of our criminal justice system. When a judge sets a bail bond of let's say, $10,000 or more. Most offenders don't have that much money. But can usually scrap together a percentage of it. So they pay a bail bond agent like Carlos 10% or $1,000 and he supplies the other $9,000. Gets it back when they appear in court, but—"

"Sometimes they don't appear," I finished.

"And the bond agent forfeits $9,000. The risky side of an otherwise lucrative business."

"So he's keenly interested in seeing they do."

"Which is where you come in."

"The wheels of justice and democracy working hand in hand."

"And the grease of capitalism to keep it moving smoothly."

"Life, liberty, and the pursuit of villains."

"Think of yourself as a personal motivator."

"A bounty hunter."

He nodded.

"If you're old school. The new, politically correct term is bail enforcement and fugitive recovery agent," he said. "When you…uh, escort them in, Carlos pays us 20% of the bond, which for him, is better than losing the whole bundle. You'll get 15% and I take 5% since you're working under my P.I. license."

He gave me a sheet of paper with information.

"Jimmie Parker is a Gulf War vet out on a $50,000 bond for armed robbery who has jumped bail. Didn't show for a recent hearing and is now off the grid. Trial starts in three weeks and if Jimmie doesn't show Carlos forfeits $40,000. So Carlos has revoked the bond, which means Jimmie needs to be apprehended and escorted back to jail. You got a place to stay?"

"Yes, sir. Headed there next."

I gave him a piece of paper with the address and my cell phone number."

"Got a gun?"

I nodded.

"A 9mm semi-automatic."

"Good. I need to make a photo I.D. for you."

He snapped a picture of me with his cell phone.

"I'll overnight the I.D. And here's Jimmie's last known address."

He handed me his business card along with a piece of paper. I stood and shook his hand.

"Thank you, sir."

"Call me if you get stuck."

"Yes, sir."

I looked over my shoulder as I walked down the driveway towards the street. In an upstairs window, Samantha had pushed aside a curtain and was watching me. I waved and the curtain closed quickly.

Ah, Sterling. Smooth with the ladies.

~TWO~

It was a two-mile walk from Glenn Howard's home to the edge of Centerville's commercial district where I caught a metro bus. And then a 90 minute ride of starts and stops to downtown Dayton. Probably only take me around 25 minutes in a car. But I didn't have one and didn't expect to anytime soon. I would de-myth the image of bounty hunting as an exciting, glamorous lifestyle as I hauled in my prisoner riding on the city metro bus.

I called Mom on my cell phone during the ride. She was packing boxes to move from a home she had just sold near Wright Patterson Air Force Base to a duplex in Centerville. After 30 years of marriage, Dad left her for a younger woman. She was the main reason I was here.

"Are you eating?" she asked.

"Of course, Mom," I said. "Breathing too."

"Uh, huh."

"In fact, to celebrate your joyous occasion, I downed an entire Happy Meal in one swallow."

"You always had a good sense of humor. The sarcasm is new."

"I'm branching out."

"Me too. Can't wait to tell you more about it."

The note in her voice surprised me. I expected to hear hurt, anger and bitterness. Instead there was a tinge of excitement. Had she won the lottery? Bought a dog? Already in another relationship? Seemed a bit early for that kind of rebound but who knows? After a few more minutes of small talk I promised to help her on moving day and hung up.

The bus ride ended at the metro bus terminal in the middle of downtown Dayton. Although small, Dayton presented itself as a thriving, cosmopolitan city. On the way through we passed a new, high-rise cultural arts center with an entire front of sparkling glass. A number of attractively renovated buildings were sprinkled randomly among the original, turn of the century ones. There was even a line of luxury condos tucked along the Great Miami River that wound around the city on its way south to Cincinnati and the Ohio River.

I hiked east along Fifth Street carrying the duffle

bag with some of my belongings. Planned to have the rest shipped when I was settled. I passed through a trendy commercial district that catered to the up and coming. Young professionals wearing business casual, ate lunch at bistros, browsed novelty boutiques, and snacked at coffee and dessert shops. Next to the business district was a residential enclave of refurbished, historical homes. A luxurious lifestyle of urban renewal.

But the landscape changed drastically when I crossed east of Keowee, a main street that ran north and south through downtown like an economic dividing line.

Neighborhoods of historical homes, once proud and distinctive in architecture, now crumbled in neglect and the press of gravity. People loitered on the street and lounged in doorways. Out of the opened doors of a few neighborhood bars spilled music, smoke, the scent of beer and raucous laughter. Snatches of happiness in the midst of a depressed environment.

Had seen similar scenes in Iraq and always considered it an effect of war. But here it was in a democratic, free market environment. Where everyone had an opportunity to make a better life. And yet, for whatever reason, some were denied.

And I wondered. Did war cause human misery or was it only a symptom of something else? A subtle enemy, perhaps, working within the shadows of human relationships to create conflict. Inciting a battle that raged within and captured the human heart.

It was a fleeting thought that I pushed away with a laugh.

C'mon Sterling. You're only 28 years old. Way too young to grow all sappy and sentimental.

I'd been having lots of second thoughts since my honorable navy discharge. Random speculations on life I had no time for a month ago. But to be expected. Leaving the military for civilian life was a big, life changing decision. No sense replaying it over and over now. I'd made the decision and it was done. Time to move on.

The scenery gradually transitioned from consumer business to industrial and residential. With industrial and residential mingling as odd consorts and the occupancy rate of both probably less than 50%. I was looking for Maple Street, which ran north and south between Fifth and Fourth Streets.

I turned right when I reached it and paused just beyond the intersection to survey the neighborhood. The street didn't extend beyond Fifth or Fourth Street so it was only around 300 yards long and I had a pretty good view of all the houses on it. About 10 or so.

A row of six identical streets east and west of Maple created a small contained, residential neighborhood surrounded by crumbling warehouses and old, dirty looking industrial businesses. An intimate sense of privacy marred by the overwhelming despair of poverty and deterioration.

Two houses on the street were exceptions. The windows had been replaced and the clapboard siding painted within the last few years. I couldn't make out the house numbers, but if I estimated correctly, one was 214, the address I was looking for. The other was two doors down from it.

In fact, a young man at the house two doors down was cleaning up after just replacing the support beams on his front porch cover with new ones. In an odd contrast, a long, low height, storage warehouse took up a third of the opposite side of street.

Two houses next door to the warehouse on the south side looked abandoned, but each had a yard sign. One announcing a public auction sale and the other a political sign that read, *Paul Mitchell for City Council.* It included the photo of a handsome young man I assumed was Paul. One other house south of the two abandoned houses appeared occupied, but showed no present sign of activity.

A neighborhood with potential. Close to downtown, but small and isolated. On the other hand, seclusion could be a bad thing.

"Yo, Homey. You lost or something?"

I turned to face three teenagers. The one speaking was obviously the Alpha male. The other two—one big and the other small—his adoring audience that snickered and snorted on cue. All three wore expensive, name brand basketball shoes, t-shirts conveying various slogans and beltless, baggie jeans that sagged well below their boxer shorts. I resisted the urge to reach out and pull them up.

"Not lost, but searching. Can you tell me the meaning of life?"

I smiled with a look of naïve sincerity. Friendly, new kid on the block. Was I mocking him or just completely clueless? Probably hard for him to determine in a first encounter. And didn't matter to him anyway because he was stirring up trouble for no reason. Maybe bored. Maybe proving himself. Maybe his chosen path to enlightenment.

Alpha was probably seventeen or eighteen, a couple of inches shorter than me, but considerably wider. He grinned too, but it wasn't friendly. And he took a menacing step forward and narrowed his eyes. A bad guy imitation picked up from TV and movies. He moved in a way to flex his muscles and I noted there was an ample supply for flexing.

"Questions about life and death be my specialty...if you get my meaning."

He took another intimidating step towards me and I obliged with a step back and a relaxed, pleasant smile. A passive move in response to his aggression. Symbolic acquiescence to domination. When your adversary is over confident, he makes mistakes. And in this case my look was deceptive. Because I was in ready position.

"Along with delivering a touchy-feely, neighborhood welcome," I said.

His smile took a cruel turn as he crushed his right fist into the palm of his left hand.

"Might say it hits the spot."

"And leaves quite an impression."

"ER docs call me a real knockout."

"And don't mean your rugged good looks."

His smile widened and he nodded. Confidence growing. Had me just where he wanted me—which is where I wanted him.

"Well, I'm actually just looking for an address...let's see, it's written on a piece of paper."

I put my hand in my duffle bag, searching.

"No, wait, I remember it's 214. Hey, I think that's it right there."

I nodded at the closer one of the two houses that defied the neighborhood deterioration and shifted slightly to the balls of my feet. Alpha noticed and hesitated. His small, dark eyes flashed a cunning, drug-like haze that probably lessened his intellectual performance. But his street smarts were on automatic.

He glanced around the neighborhood and I did the same. There was an expensive, foreign made car parked on the street along with a U-Rent moving truck, but no activity at the moment. And the man working on his porch had finished cleaning up and gone inside. Alpha shifted his attention back to me.

"You know, you don't even rate my time. Tiny, show this Homey how we welcome to the hood."

Tiny was actually not tiny, but huge—around 6' 5" and expansive in all directions.

He ambled toward me with the relaxed confidence of someone accustomed to easily man handling others. So he looked quite surprise when he was a step away, reaching out to grab my arm, and rather than recoiling in fear as expected, I stepped forward and shoved the duffle bag hard into his stomach. Had he been ready, it might have simply bounced off. But he wasn't and stepped back to keep his balance. Except I stuck my leg behind his to trip him and he fell backward like a mighty oak.

His smaller counterpart tried vainly to catch him, but there was too much weight and too much momentum. They crashed hard with the smaller guy getting the worst of it. He got up slower than Tiny who scrambled to his feet ready for full assault. But Alpha held his hand up for him to stop.

"You brave, Homey," he said. "Or stupid. Cause I say what do and don't go around here."

"Does and doesn't," I said.

"Huh?"

"Good communication is the key to effective leadership. I say what does and doesn't go on around here. If you expect me to understand your threat, you need to be clear."

He didn't get the grammar lesson, but he understood the mocking tone of my voice. No hiding it this time. I didn't normally provoke an adversary.

But at the moment I was hot, tired and in a no-tolerance for punks mood.

"There also be quite a few serious accidents around here."

"Figured that when I saw the three of you. Or are you guys presenting a new version of dumb-dumb and dumber?"

He smiled viciously and pulled a long, wicked looking knife from his pocket.

"You real funny, Homey. Since you so funny, guess me and my friend Dice here gonna cut-up with you."

He tossed the knife in practiced grabs from hand to hand and made smooth, cutting sweeps through the air with each. I pulled the 9mm semi-automatic from my duffle bag and waved it casually in his direction.

"Sure. You and Dice. Me and my boring friend, Millie. Should be hilarious."

He stopped, weighed his options and realized there weren't any. He put the knife back in his pocket and smiled again. The malice it radiated should have melted my heart into a fearful mush.

But it didn't. Malice and fear were just two of the many emotions you managed in combat. Too much sway on either side jeopardized clear decision-making and could be costly.

"Gonna wish you hadn't done that, Homey."

I gave him a friendly smile that said no hard feelings.

"Disagree on that, but I embrace your diversity of thought. Cause right now, I'm really glad I did. But I appreciate your neighborly offer of such warm hospitality."

"See you around, Homey."

"Have a nice day, gentlemen."

He flipped his middle finger at me as they walked away. Had the last word after all if you include non-verbal forms of communication. I sighed and headed towards 214. Ah, home sweet home.

~THREE~

As I walked down Maple Street the quiet neighborhood suddenly sprang to life. From the house several doors down two couples, thirtyish, emerged carrying boxes and furniture, which they carried into the back of the U-Rent truck. Then a man wearing a sport jacket with a realtor logo emerged from 214. He looked mid-40's, medium build and paunchy. His dark brown hair, meticulously starched in place, suspiciously lacked any gray.

He gave me a brief, emotionless smile.

"How are you?" he asked without pausing for me to answer. Apparently on a mission. He climbed into the expensive, foreign made sedan, started it up and drove away.

"Doing great," I said to the empty street. "Thanks for asking. Nice talking to you."

Another contemplative question popped into my mind: Is it better to be hated or ignored? I filed it away for later consideration.

I stepped on the porch of 214, which was littered with glass from a shattered front window and knocked on a screen door. Behind it, the front door was partially open. A shrill woman's voice rang out.

"Told you, I'm not selling!"

"Not buying, renting. Jack Sterling. Called about your apartment?"

An older woman appeared at the door. Seventies. Short and thin, but with fire in her intelligent blues eyes. Seeing me, she pulled up with a look of surprise.

"Look out of place for this neighborhood."

"Looks can be deceiving."

"Around here they're pretty dependable. Thought you was that phony real estate agent coming back. Wants to buy my home and won't take no for an answer. Man his age with not a speck of gray in his hair. What else he hiding?"

She opened the door and waved me into a small foyer nodding towards a pile of business cards on a small table.

"Bought Mary Jane's house a few doors down. Now he's pestering me and Norma who lives next door. Neither of us interested. Not sure about Mike and Sondra Thompson on the other side of Norma. Or the Williams across the street and down a ways. All that's left of us. Course Mary Jane was losing it. Had to fetch her from wandering around downtown several times. Miracle she didn't wander into the river and float to Cincinnati."

I handed Stella six hundred dollar bills and a fifty.

"My deposit and first month's rent."

It left a hundred in my wallet. And modest savings at the Navy base credit union in California that I'd transfer when I had a local bank account. Might have to stretch it out so I was living cheap and this was the lowest rent I found. Now I knew why. It came with neighborhood thugs ready to maim on demand. Even offered a few slices without asking.

She looked at the money then back at me.

"You don't want to see it first and then decide?"

"Figured if it wasn't okay you wouldn't rent it. See it now if you don't mind."

Taking a chance it wasn't a dump. Not that it mattered since my options were limited. But it turned out to be clean and comfortable. A small flat above a detached, two-car garage next to her house. The garage looked ancient, but sturdy. A gray, cinder block building with a side entrance door and inside steps up to the apartment above. A converted attic. I thought of the potential drive by shootings and decided that short of an underground bunker, it was as secure as you could hope for in this neighborhood. I might also consider bullet proof sleepwear.

It was no frills as expected. A compact kitchen, tiny eating area, living room and full size bed squeezed into one open space. With only a small bathroom offering a separate room of privacy. Complete with worn, but clean furniture. It would do.

Stella handed me a set of keys.

"My husband converted it before he passed to give us extra income. Most renters don't make it past a couple of months. Guess you know why.

Sorry I was a bit short."

"But spunky," I said.

"Save the flattery, Kid. You got a job?"

"Just hired."

She hesitated, deciding whether or not to share any more with me. Guess my trustworthy look convinced her it was okay.

"Rotten kid, Jerome tossed a rock through my front window. Know it was him and for no cause. Just plain mean. Him and his two misfit friends, Tiny and Bo. Say this neighborhood is their turf."

"You call the police?"

"Yeah. Came, did a lot of head nodding. You know, humor the batty old women. Filled out a report and then nothing. Probably used it to wipe his..."

She stopped. Unsure of my sensibilities.

"Filthy shoes?" I finished.

Stella grinned. Then her face set in fierce resolve.

"This house is all I got. Not giving in without a fight!"

I admired her determination. But if her house was the prize for a gang and it came to a fight, she'd lose. Not sure even Millie and I would make a difference.

~FOUR~

Why would anyone want to buy a worthless home in a depressed neighborhood? Especially one with a gang. I wondered.

Stella let me borrow her American made, compact car parked in the garage beneath me. High in years, but low in miles, it was a four cylinder putt-putt that blazed from zero to thirty in 60 seconds and shuttered when you surpassed 65 miles an hour. I named it Flash. But still better than the metro bus, so I owed Stella something.

I took one of the realtor business cards off the table in her foyer. The name read Chalmers Realty, which was located in a small shopping strip in the suburban city of Kettering. A narrow storefront sandwiched between a grocery store and a tanning salon.

A young woman, probably 18-20, dressed Gothic, sat at the front desk. Black pants and black, rock band t-shirt with tattoos on both arms. Black hair, dark mascara and pasty white skin. Off-set with bright red lipstick, bright red fingernail polish, shiny rings on every finger of her left hand and eight or nine bracelets on her right wrist. Morning prep time had to run an hour long at the least.

An alternative magazine lay open on her desk, and she glanced at it while typing on a desktop computer with an office phone wedged to her ear in a conversation with "Yo and Dude." The magazine article featured the picture of a male rock star. His identity masked behind white make-up, black mascara around the eyes and long, dark hair—maybe a wig?

A cell phone was in easy reach and she paused occasionally to send a text. A multi-tasker.

Her chair backed up against a six-foot high modular wall separating an office area that extended behind her. There was a waiting room of sorts in front of her desk—a coffee table with a couple of magazines and a few chairs next to the front, plate glass window. Did I really want to sit in a seat with my back against a plate glass window—on display to the world?

Deciding no, I stood with a smile on my face and stared at her while she ignored me. Staring at people is generally unnerving, but this girl didn't intimidate easy. A heavy dose of insolence will do that for you. So I stepped forward…a little closer into her personal space. She looked up and spoke into the phone.

"Hold on a sec, k?"

She punched a button and looked at me.

"Yeah?"

With such highly refined public relations skills, I was amazed customers weren't lined up out the door.

I put on my best disarming smile, innocent, yet playful.

"I'm looking for luxurious real estate and by the looks of it I just hit the mother lode."

She rolled her eyes and spoke into the phone.

"Call you back."

She hung up and focused her entire attention on me. This time, along with attitude, I saw keen intelligence. How did I ever miss that attitude the first time?

"Alternative dress doesn't mean I'm a dim wit. You wanna be a clown, go join the circus. What do you want?"

So much for the charming, indirect approach. Time for direct.

"Is Gary Chalmers in?"

"Let me check."

She turned halfway in her seat and called back.

"Hey, Gary, there's a guy here, thinks he's a comedian, wants to see you. Are you in?"

A voice called from the back.

"Is he funny?"

"He thinks so."

"What do you think?"

"You both know I'm standing right here, right? Listening to your conversation?" I asked.

Neither of them acknowledged me. Maybe I had the power of invisibility?

"He's cute if you like Boy Scouts. Not my type," said Gothic Girl."

"What if I was a walking dead Boy Scout?" I countered.

Our conversation was growing more peculiar by the moment. Now I was identifying myself as dead to be recognized as alive and present. Proof that opposites attract or aliens live among us?

Gothic Girl refocused and scrutinized me carefully. Her eyes narrowing to a naughty gleam and her mouth twisting into a deviant grin. A creepy interest that gave me the chills. Like fresh killed game being sized up for field dressing. Then she was back to the present with a dismissive, bracelet jingling wave of her hand.

"Naw."

Chalmers brought the conversation back to business.

"Boy Scout got a name?"

She raised her eyebrows at me.

"Jack Sterling."

She leaned around again.

"Jack Sterling."

"Never heard of him."

She turned and looked at me.

"Sorry, he's in a meeting."

I smiled at her.

"You two have obviously developed a highly refined method of qualifying clients and then communicating through subliminal messaging. So thank you for your time."

I leaned around the corner and raised my voice so Gary heard me.

"Just tell Gary that Jack Sterling from Lincoln Financial Group was here to discuss property. I'll try someone else."

I had read an article about Lincoln Financial in a regional magazine someone left on the metro bus yesterday. It was a company owned by the multi-billionaire Lincoln family from Columbus—a name recognized throughout state. James Lincoln started out with a mini-market that grew into a chain of mini-markets. And as the chain expanded, the company grew into a financial investment empire with business holdings across multiple states. I wasn't particularly interested in the magazine or the article, but it passed the time during my bus ride. And what I had considered useless information was suddenly, strategically useful. I made a mental note for my future book on the exciting life of a private investigator. When you lack power, leverage influence.

Gary Chalmers appeared before I reached the door.

"Mr. Sterling. Hey, it's great to meet you. C'mon back to my office."

His office was a cubicle past two other empty cubicles beyond Gothic girl's six foot barrier. It was right next to the bathroom which, depending on your perspective, could be good or bad. He gestured for me to sit in a padded chair with the look of someone searching his memory.

"Have we met?"

"Not officially. I just moved into an apartment on Maple Street."

He snapped his fingers as the memory clicked in.

"Stella's garage apartment. Don't look like the type you'd expect in that neighborhood."

"I've heard. Bank account says different."

He nodded.

"I could afford a nicer office than this. But I focus on service rather than overhead."

"Like investing in a warm, friendly and helpful receptionist?"

He smiled and lifted his hands, palms up in surrender.

"Family. What are you gonna do? So, how can I help you?"

"Interested in the two homes across from Stella's house. Know who bought them?"

He shrugged.

"Sold at an auction."

"What about Mary Jane's house, the lady moving out the other day?"

"A client of mine."

"When's he moving in?"

"Never said it was a he."

"He, she or it."

"I close the deal and record it on the books. I don't pry into a client's personal agenda."

"Same client who wants to buy Stella's and Norma's house?"

"I have more than one client."

"More than one client interested in that neighborhood?"

He narrowed his eyes shrewdly.

"I thought you wanted to talk property."

"I am talking property."

"Seems more like an investigation."

"Fact finding."

He stood to signal that the meeting was over.

"Well, I'm all out of facts. But when you're ready to drop some money on the table, come back and see me. That's a conversation that interests me."

I didn't budge.

"That neighborhood is not what I'd call family friendly. So what's the attraction?"

"Full of potential. Close to downtown. A new, multi-million dollar cultural performing arts center and minor league baseball stadium down the street. Growing interest in urban renewal."

I'd seen the new performing arts center from the bus yesterday. It was certainly impressive architecture that demonstrated a commitment to downtown revitalization. Had also seen ads for Dayton's minor league baseball team—single A farm club for Cincinnati's major league team.

"I suggest you find an agent that specializes in that neighborhood. I just represent a few random investors. Good luck."

He stood and offered his hand, so I stood and shook it.

"Thanks for your time."

~FIVE~

The address I had for Jimmie was a modest, brick ranch in the suburban neighborhood of Kettering. It was on a street lined with clone, brick ranches on little square lots with narrow driveways and one car garages. None of the garages looked like they were used for cars. The ones with open doors were crammed with junk.

Small trees populated some of the tiny front yards, but most were bare for lack of green space. Homes were personalized through window treatments, stylish front doors and varied landscaping.

I hid the 9mm semi-automatic gun under my untucked shirttail. Had a small roll of duct tape in my pocket for handcuffs. Didn't expect to find Jimmie here, but was trained to always put preparation before expectations.

A small, elderly woman with reddish, hair that leaned strongly towards orange, answered the door. She had gentle eyes and a kind smile. The mother you'd expect of a saint, not a felon.

"Mrs. Parker?"

"Yes?"

"I'm looking for Jimmie. Is he home?"

Dumb question, but not sure what else to ask. Maybe, "Can Jimmie come out to play?" Or, "What time does Jimmie usually get home after a robbery?"

She smiled like it was a perfectly natural question.

"I'm sorry, he's not here. Would you like to come inside?"

Could be an act of feigned innocence. A mother's instinct to protect her child was an unbreakable bond. But if she was pretending she deserved a best actress award.

I stepped into a small, but comfortably furnished living room with a worn couch, love seat and arm chair gathered around a coffee table. Everything was clean, comfortable and 20 years out of date, including the color TV with a picture tube rather than flat screen broadcasting a game show. The game show host was warm and friendly and two beautiful women posed gracefully to showcase the prizes. Superficial happiness with gleaming smiles, glittering lights and enthusiastic contestants whose hopes were dashed when their price was not right.

Hope without purpose. Accumulation without accomplishment. Gain without productivity. And hiding behind all those smiles? Who knew?

Completely opposite of my life. The path to becoming a Navy SEAL was physically and mentally grueling and pushed human endurance beyond all boundaries. Only a handful of guys that started made it through all the way. And when you did, you were bonded like family. It didn't get any easier moving forward either.

Constant risk. Exposure to the harshest elements. Adrenalin pumping action. But what I did mattered and provided a clear sense of purpose. But now it was gone. Now, I was a little lost.

Mrs. Parker nodded at a cup of tea and plate of cheese and crackers on the coffee table.

"Would you care for some green tea?" she asked.

"Sure," I said taking a seat on the couch while she went to the kitchen.

She returned with a cup that I sipped and raised my eyes in appreciation. A taste of lemon and honey combined into a zesty flavor.

"Sweet and sour," she said proudly. "My own blend."

I took another sip then put the cup down on a coaster on the coffee table.

"Mrs. Parker, have you heard from Jimmie lately?" I asked.

Her face grew sad.

"Not since he...since he got into trouble. Before that he came by all the time."

"So he didn't live here."

"No, but all his mail came here. Still does. Would you like to see his room?"

"Sure," I replied. She hadn't even asked who I was or what I wanted with Jimmie. Maybe she didn't want to know or already had a good idea. Self-denial takes strange forms.

She led me down a short hallway to where three small bedrooms were clustered together. The master bedroom was hers, the second looked like a guest room and the last one—where we stopped—was Jimmie's.

The room was immaculate and appropriately decorated for a 12 year old boy. From the small, twin bed with a caped, super hero bedspread, baseball card collection on the student desk next to the window, and posters of famous baseball and basketball stars on the wall. A shrine to simpler, happier days. Maybe why she was so cheerful. She was blocking the present from her mind and living in the past. Where Jimmie was forever, her precious, little boy no matter what.

The poster of a famous, long haired, rock'n roll star jamming on an electric guitar was the only hint towards a possibly, rebellious adolescence. Not something I related to. My father had ruled our home with the iron fist of a military command so there was little expression of unique personalities or modern teenage culture. And since I enlisted in the Navy at 17, a good part of adolescence was traded for adulthood. I wondered briefly if I had missed something and decided it did no good to speculate on it now.

"The other room belonged to his sister Carol," said Mrs. Parker. "I turned it into a guest room a few years ago."

"Were they close?" I asked.

"Not really. She was six years older than Jimmie and they lived in different worlds."

"She still around? You see her much?"

It looked like Mrs. Parker lived a quiet, lonely life.

"No. Has a family and salvage yard down in Lebanon that keeps her busy. Funny how you can live close to someone and not see them much. Sometimes I go down and watch the grandkids."

"What about Jimmie's father?"

"Moved to Arizona with another woman after our divorce. Not sure, which came first. Woman or the divorce. Jimmie was young. His father sent birthday cards and gift certificates for Christmas until Jimmie turned 18. Didn't hear much from him after that."

She looked wistful for a moment. Like the memory brought her painfully up to the present. She pointed to a picture on a small table.

"That's Jimmie in the sixth grade."

It was a smiling, redheaded boy with freckles wearing a Boy Scout uniform. A smile of innocence, free of worries, looking forward to a good life ahead. Today he was probably mid to late 30's. I wondered what his smile was like now.

"Jimmie was a good boy. Always on the quiet side. I know war changed him, but he wouldn't do what they said he did."

She spoke with determination. I doubted even the store security video footage would convince her otherwise.

"When's the last time you heard from him?" I asked.

She thought for a minute.

"He called me after his arrest. And I spoke to his public defender. Can't remember his name, but he arranged for Jimmie's release…"

"On bail bond," I finished.

"Yes."

"And now he's disappeared. Any idea where he is?"

"He never talks much about himself."

She seemed apologetic like suddenly realizing she should have more concern for her son and felt guilty about it.

"I do have a telephone number for him."

She handed me a piece of paper with the number and smiled as she safely retreated back to fonder memories.

"Jimmie was a hard worker and a faithful son. He always brought me flowers on Mother's Day and took me out to dinner. Even this last Mother's Day."

"But you haven't seen him recently."

"No...not recently. But that will change when this misunderstanding is settled."

"I'm sure it will."

There is no refuting a mother's love. I politely excused myself, left, and called the number she gave me when I was in the car. It was disconnected. Now what?

I called Frank's house for help and Samantha answered.

"Hey gorgeous."

"Don't patronize me."

"Wow. Big word. Even for a 13 or 14 year old. Good looking AND smart."

There was a slight pause as she searched for a snappy comeback, but couldn't think of one.

"Need help don't you."

"A little direction."

"Thought you learned navigation as a SEAL."

"That was geographic. This is investigatory."

"Spin it how you like. Fact is, you're lost."

"I prefer slightly wandering."

"Yeah, right."

A slight pause and then Frank's voice.

"Problem?"

"Sir, I'm lost. The address you gave me for Jimmie is a bust. His mom's address that he never used."

"His mom give you anything?"

"A phone number that is disconnected."

"You any good at conducting online searches?"

"Guess not. Don't even have a computer right now. Limited to my phone."

"You can access some public records online. And there are several subscription-based online information services used by the legal community and law enforcement agencies that provide even more. But a bit pricey so I've never subscribed myself. Without access to any of those tools you'll have to go old school."

"Such as?"

"Reverse telephone directory at the public library. Might give you an address that goes with the number. And check his name in public records downtown at the Montgomery County Courthouse. Might pick up leads there too. Let me know how it goes."

I hung up realizing the hard part to this case would not be apprehending Jimmie. It would be finding him.

~SIX~

I keyed notes into my phone from the visit to Gary Chalmers and Mrs. Parker. Things said. Observations made. Fragments of speculative thoughts on what it all meant. Which could be nothing. But it helped me organize and record details. Maybe within those details I'd find threads to pull that unraveled the cloak of mystery.

I visited the downtown public library, checked the reverse phone directory and found an address attached to the telephone number Mrs. Parker gave me. It was an old apartment building in a rundown neighborhood just north of the Kettering border in the city of Dayton. A non-descript rectangle, red brick building among a group of identical, non-descript rectangle, red brick buildings.

The brick was weather stained, the gray, aluminum windows old and grimy and the gutters sagged with neglect. No frills, low rent living for life on the cheap. A transient area of drive-thru carry-outs, fast food restaurants and dollar discount stores.

The resident apartment manager was a middle-aged man with greasy, slicked backed hair and a mound of stomach who answered the door in boxer shorts, a sleeveless t-shirt and chewing on a fried chicken leg. The perfect choice for discouraging potential renters.

I flashed my new, private investigator I.D. that had arrived by courier yesterday afternoon, hoping he didn't look at it closely. He didn't. But other than knowing Jimmie paid last month's rent, the manager specialized in complete ignorance. He did however, let me into Jimmie's apartment.

In contrast to the surrounding environment it was neat and clean. But lifeless. No pictures, no keepsakes. In the bedroom closet I found a multiple selection of work clothes. Two pairs of dress pants and shirts and one suit. Several pairs of well-worn work boots, one pair of casual shoes and one pair of dress shoes. In other words, busy professional life. Not much of a social life. He and I had a lot in common.

The kitchen was typical bachelor with single servings of microwavable foods in the refrigerator. A tiny living room with a worn couch, chair with ottoman, and modest, flat-screen TV with cable hook-up. Comfortable, but stark. A place to eat and sleep. Not hang out with your friends.

    I searched a cardboard file box in the living room where he kept records. I found the title to a few years old, popular model, ¾ ton pickup truck. No lien holder was listed on the title so he must have paid cash. Maybe drained his military savings?

    I went through statements of his one major credit card. There were grocery store charges, fast food restaurants and hardware store purchases. Nothing unusual or suspicious. He carried a $2,000 balance, but made consistent payments. According to his bank statement he had no savings and $300 in checking. There were also several check stubs made out to him that noted "home remodeling" on the memo section. He wasn't getting ahead, but he was getting by. So why the robbery? Maybe trading in getting by for getting ahead?

    I knocked on the doors of other apartments, but only found one tenant home—an elderly woman on the first floor who furtively peeked out the crack in her door opened to the length of a security chain.

I gave her my best, disarming smile.

"Hello," I said. "I..."

She slammed the door shut without a word.

"Represent Publications Open House Sweepstakes and you've won!"

Two deadbolts locked into place. Note to self: disarming smile needs improvement.

I expanded my search to the neighboring apartment buildings. Nothing doing there either. But people don't live in complete isolation. Someone had to know something useful about Jimmie Parker. I just had to persist until I found the person or persons. Except I had a deadline. Jimmie's trial started in two weeks. If he didn't appear in court the bail bond money that Carlos Fernandez fronted was forfeited. Bad for Carlos and bad for me.

With a renewed sense of motivation I canvassed the local stores and businesses. There was a dry cleaner, a mini-mart, cell phone repair shop, and Chinese restaurant among others. Many of the people knew Jimmie by sight, which sounded promising. But no one had any more than a superficial interaction with him and no idea where he might be.

My last stop was Digger's Pub. There was a cozy feel to it like a warm refuge in a cold, indifferent environment. Perhaps a place for social interaction and sense of belonging?

I sat at the bar near two burly men layered in blacktop. They were eating sandwiches, drinking beer and arguing heatedly over next season's best professional football teams.

Two other guys in brown, delivery uniforms played a spirited game of darts. A man and woman shared a quiet conversation in a booth. And the bar tender, a balding man with pockmarked face, exploding gut, towel slung over his right shoulder and eye on a soap opera, slid over to me.

"What'll you have?"

"Draft," I said. "You Digger?"

He nodded affirmation as he filled a mug from the tap and placed it in front of me without taking his eyes off the TV program where two men argued heatedly over a woman.

The two men arguing over football seemed more realistic, but then soap operas were targeted to women as an entertaining form of escape, not a reflection of reality. I sipped my drink and pondered on art imitating life versus life imitating art. Was there a difference? And if so, what was it?

It led to other speculations like...which came first, the chicken or the egg? If truth is an illusion can an Illusionist lie? And what's the real value of a reality check?

I pictured the two burly men at the bar arguing over ballet—Nutcracker versus Swan Lake and chuckled to myself. Digger glanced at me and self-consciously changed to a news channel.

"Addictive aren't they?" I said.

He nodded.

"A couple of administrative assistants used to come in for lunch every day. Eat and watch the show. Before I knew it, I was hooked."

I tried to look empathetic and nodded affably.

"Habits can be hard to break. You see Jimmie lately? Got a remodeling job for him."

He shook his head.

"Not since he got in trouble with the law."

I played dumb. One of my natural skills.

"Yeah? What happened?"

"Shoplifting I think."

"Hard times?" I asked.

"Digger gave me a wry smile.

"See anyone looks like they're on easy street?"

"Money isn't everything," I said.

A trite cliché, but wanted to keep the conversation going. Digger wiped a wet spot on the bar with the towel from his shoulder.

"Jimmie managed same as most people around here. Seemed okay with it. Content."

"So what changed?"

He shrugged.

"This part of town is not a final destination for people. Everyone is just passing through on their way to something better. Change is the only constant. Need anything else?"

I slapped a bill on the bar and rose to leave.

"Nope. I'll keep looking."

Digger picked it up and put it in the cash register. Didn't offer to make change and I didn't ask for any. Big tipper that I am. Pay for the drink. Pay for information. Get nothing but a drink. Maybe I should consider bar tending.

"Good luck," he said.

I gave him a two finger salute.

"Be needing it."

Digger knew my interest in Jimmie was more than a job and I knew Digger knew more than he was telling me. Good to know we were both in the know. Now if I could just get to know what I didn't know. You know?

I glanced over my shoulder as I left and saw him switch back to the soap opera. Yep, habits can be hard to break.

~SEVEN~

I expected Mom to be alone and overwhelmed on moving day and myself, the rescuing young hero. But to my surprise her duplex bustled with activity— full of people laughing and talking but smoothly and efficiently moving. They all seemed to know each other, be completely at ease and enjoying a task usually marked by drudgery. I was the only family relative, but felt like the stranger.

Mom rushed over when she saw me. Dressed in jeans and an Ohio State sweat shirt. Her dark brown, shoulder length hair was sprinkled with gray and pulled back into a pony tail. And her brown eyes sparkled with an energy that seemed new and different. For a woman recently divorced after 30 years of marriage, she looked incredibly vibrant. I wondered if she was already seeing someone new.

She introduced me to everyone helping who all possessed the same energy she did. Maybe they were all seeing someone new.

I paired up with Terrance Williams, an African-American man who at around 6' 7" and well over

250 pounds, had football somewhere in his past. Jeff Loo and Warren Dunn were the other two men helping. Jeff was a lithe, Asian-American half the size of Terrance and everything about Warren said white, middle class, computer geek. About as different as three men could be and yet they were totally into a shared conversation. I can usually hold my own in most conversations. Unfortunately for me, this one was about religion.

"Confucius say that he who knows all the answers has not been asked all the questions," said Jeff.

Warren looked peeved.

"What does that have to do with what we're talking about?"

"Nothing. But every good Asian-American is expected to quote Confucius. Part of our rich, ancestral heritage."

Warren went from peeved to confused.

"Confucius was Chinese. You're Korean."

Jeff smiled and nodded.

"So. We all look alike anyway."

Humor probably wasn't Warren's strong suit, but he gave it shot.

"And is martial arts part of your rich, ancestral heritage too?"

"Nope. Genetic."

"So back on topic," said Terrence. "Does God change His mind when we pray?"

"God is immutable and sovereign," said Warren. "And prayer should not be viewed as divine leverage. Like a tool that bends God to do our will."

"Meaning God's gonna do what He's gonna do no matter what?" asked Terrance.

"Then why pray if it doesn't make a difference?" asked Jeff.

"That's the mystery," said Warren. "It does make a difference. We just don't know how or why."

"Or when," said Terrence. "I'm praying for things God hasn't answered yet."

"Well, if you're praying for a thirty-three inch waist, maybe the answer is no," said Jeff.

"Kinda like your prayer to grow up to six two?"

"Why would I pray for that? Big things come in small packages."

"Yeah. God being like a celestial Santa Claus and all," said Terrence. "So if God already knows what we're about to ask, that mean He knows His answer too?"

"Yeah, like...can God create a rock too big for Him to lift?" added Jeff.

"Guys, can we please not get sidetracked on sophomoric discussions?" asked Warren. "It's difficult for our finite minds to grasp the full magnitude of God. In 2 Kings chapter 20, when Hezekiah was sick and the prophet Isaiah told him he was going to die, Hezekiah prayed and God healed him."

Without thinking I blurted out.

"So did God change his mind? Or did he just tell Hezekiah he was going to die, knowing that Hezekiah would ask for healing and when he did, God would say yes? And if so, what does that mean because isn't God big on free will?"

They all looked at me dumbfounded. Like the deaf mute had just been healed.

"God knows the choices we will make, but it doesn't mean he influences the decision," said Warren.

"So we pray with no idea what the effect is," said Jeff.

"But that it does have an effect," said Terrance.

"Yes," said Warren.

Terrance looked at me with a grin.

"So what do you think, Jack?"

I shrugged.

"Not much for religion. Guess I don't have a prayer."

Terrence started to reply, but a group of women and children burst through the door carrying food. A flurry of activities set the stage for a meal and conversation shifted to weather, sports and family for which I was glad.

I was introduced to Terrance's wife, Natalie and their 5 kids, Warren's wife Linda and their 3 kids, and Jeff's girlfriend, Lee-Ann. And a strikingly beautiful young woman named Beth that I had to consciously not stare at, but discreetly noticed wore no wedding band.

There was a sense of warmth and belonging in the group I found compelling. But all the talk about God and church that they naturally sprinkled into their conversation was foreign and uncomfortable for me. I was relieved when we finished and I could leave. I was glad this religion thing worked for Mom, but for me? No thank you.

~EIGHT~

The sun dipped half-way below the horizon when I got home. Dark etched across the neighborhood as fingers of waning sunlight stabbed into the sky. Shadows spread across the landscape creating an effect that contrasted sharply to Norma's house next door to Stella. It was engulfed in flames.

A small crowd watched fire fighters battle the blaze. Stella stood next to Norma, holding her for support. The looks on their faces were hopeful until the roof and second floor collapsed to the ground. Then they bowed their heads silently and went into Stella's home.

As the flames died down the crowd dispersed. Either the fire fighters had finally gained control or the fire was simply running out of fuel. Guess it depended on whether you were a half-full or half-empty glass type of person. Either way the house was gone.

I joined Mike Thompson, who lived on the other side of Norma, and was also standing in the crowd. He had moved his young family from Louisville for an assembly line job at a local manufacturing plant that produced pick-up trucks. When the plant closed several years ago, he took classes at the local Community College and landed a CNC equipment operator job at a machine tooling company. But he was laid off that job a couple months ago and was using the time to fix up his house. He looked sad and relieved at the same time. Sad for Norma. Glad the fire hadn't jumped over to his house.

"Any idea what happened?"

"Nope," Mike said. "I was scraping paint on the other side of my house and couldn't see anything. Started to smell smoke and heard the sirens. By then the fire was going full throttle."

Mike nodded at Jerome and his two sidekicks who stood apart from the crowd, and unlike everyone else, laughed and joked.

"Can see them having a hand in it."

Jerome caught my eye and gave a mock salute. Just a random act or did he know I was former military? Hard to say. I was certain the street had its own communication network. And a good reminder too. Jerome might not score high on academic proficiency tests, but when it came to street smarts, there was an intelligent cunning that put him at the top of the class.

"And their reason?"

"None needed 'cept to be mean," Mike said.

I nodded.

"Heard that before."

The perverted joy some people took in the tragedy of others. There was an in your face sense of victory in Jerome's behavior. Seen it many times, but always facing a foreign enemy. Not at home. And that was the hard part. I knew protecting freedom included the rights of those who didn't appreciate it. Even trampled on the ideals I fought to protect. But it sickened me to see it.

Our SEAL team had a code of integrity and honor that gave my life purpose and meaning. But now it was gone and I wasn't sure where I fit in.

It was all still pretty fresh. And I knew not to trust my emotions...that I was mourning a loss. But still couldn't help feeling cheated.

The crowd slowly dispersed and the fire fighters put away their equipment.

"Homes on this street are dropping like flies," said Mike.

"On the bright side, look at all the privacy you have."

"Yeah, if I can last to enjoy it. Missed a couple of house payments and already getting foreclosure warnings from the bank."

He shook his head.

"Can't see how a home on this street is anything but an unwanted burden for a bank."

"You'd think," I agreed.

Norma would stay with Stella tonight and maybe a few more days. But Stella wasn't one to share personal space long term. Which made me wonder. Did anything last?

~NINE~

In the morning, I walked through the smoldering remains of Norma's house with Bob Mitchell, a Dayton City fire investigator. He had thick, salty hair, serious brown eyes that had seen many fires and strong looking hands that had fought them. He commented as we walked carefully on the ground floor. There were several spots where the wooden flooring was burnt away revealing the basement below.

"These old houses are like tinder boxes. Ancient electrical wiring never designed to handle the pull of modern appliances. Add computers and all the other technology plugged in and you have a disaster waiting to happen."

He shook his head sadly as he walked, kicking debris with his boots. Twirls of smoke spiraled in the air marked by a pungent odor of charred remains. Blackened furniture in skeleton form, molten metal appliances, and stark portions of wall framing standing in stubborn defiance.

"Started at the stove in the kitchen."

"Know how?" I asked.

"My guess, something flammable in the electric eye. Norma was frying chicken in the skillet last night. The grease caught and it spread from there while she was out back hanging up wet clothes on a clothes line to dry."

"Something what flammable and how'd it get there?"

He smiled ruefully.

"That's the million dollar question. Norma said she had a stack of mail on the kitchen counter. The kitchen window was open. A breeze could have blown a piece of paper into the eye. Or maybe hot grease splattered from the skillet to the paper and caught it on fire."

He shrugged like it was a stretch, but had nothing better to offer.

"Sounds like a fairy tale to me. Aren't they supposed to have happy endings?"

"Norma wasn't in the house. That's a happy ending."

"Who called 911?"

"Stella. And she had to hold Norma back from going in with a garden hose. By the time we arrived, the question wasn't if the house would survive, but if it would take other houses with it."

"So what's the ruling?"

"Going with accident."

"What about Jerome and his sidekicks?"

Bob Mitchell squinted at me and shielded his eyes from a bright, morning sun.

"What about them?"

"Agile young man could easily climb through the open window and help paper into the hot electric eye? In and out in a flash."

"What's the motive?"

"Establishing his turf. Send a message to everyone in the neighborhood. Kid like that...maybe just pure evil."

Bob thought it over.

"He's also pretty smart. And that's taking a big risk. Can't see him doing that without a good reason."

"Doesn't mean there isn't one."

Bob grunted as he kicked a kitchen chair out of the way. The cushion was burned off, but the rest of the metal frame was just charred black.

"How about Norma did it to claim insurance?"

"What's her motive?"

"Ticket out of the neighborhood. Might get more from the insurance company than a buyer."

"Even though she tried to put the fire out with a garden hose?"

"A little drama to sell it. Maybe she's the one who's smarter than we think."

"You believe that?"

"I've seen stranger."

He had a point. Seen some strange stuff too. But Norma's grief looked pretty genuine. Hard for me to believe it was an act.

"Of course, if that's the case then this is poetic justice," said Bob.

"Why?"

He pointed through a hole in the floor where the basement wall caved inward.

"Foundation has to be re-poured before you can rebuild and that will be costly. Insurance settlement won't cover it. Unless Norma has a pile of money stashed in the bank, she'll have to move anyway."

~TEN~

I stopped in at the Montgomery County Courthouse—a 10-story building on West Third Street in downtown Dayton. It was home to several Common Pleas courtrooms along with numerous government departments and agencies scattered among the various floors.

As a new sleuth, I was clueless on how to check public records. And wouldn't you know it? There were no customer service representatives waiting to assist me when I entered the building. In fact, everyone coming and going seemed to know exactly where they were coming and going to. And did so in a purposeful manner.

I on the other hand was groping. And the irony of it was not lost on me. Most certainly, groping was the specific reason some of the people were appearing in court today. A good reminder to always keep things in proper perspective and context.

After consulting the directory in the lobby I started with the real estate department. Fortunately, they were not busy and a young lady name Shonda showed me how to look through the huge plat books that showed actual property lines of all the real estate in the county. Each book represented a particular area of the county that was further broken down by neighborhoods and individual parcels of property. Fascinating, but not helpful. Although she then directed me to the Clerk of Courts where I learned who owned the property and name of the lien holder if one applied.

From there I moved to criminal & civil records, marriage & divorce records and bankruptcy & financial lien records. It was boring, tedious work that took longer because I was learning on the go. Definitely not the glamorous life of a TV private investigator.

When finished I knew Jimmie owned no real estate and had never been sued or sued anyone else. He had no marriage record, no loan on public record and never filed for bankruptcy. His mom owned the property in Kettering. And a company called Paxco LLC had purchased the homes sold on Maple street. So far, not much that was helpful. But

I chose to be hopeful. Always good to maintain a positive attitude when homelessness is on the line.

Glenn Howard had supplied the name of Jimmie's arresting officer—Detective Mark Thornton. Since the Dayton Police Headquarters was just across the street from the Courthouse, I took a chance Detective Thornton might be in his office. A chance he might have something useful to tell me. And a chance if he did, he would share it with me. For a trained Navy SEAL like myself, risk is just another day at the office.

The detective division was a large room full of cubicles with five-foot partition walls and no obvious, check-in desk. The chief and assistant chief of detectives had glass offices along the wall. Their doors were closed and blinds pulled. High level detective meetings in progress. Or perhaps an afternoon nap.

I heard movement and phone conversations going on, but decided wandering the room and poking my head into cubicles where the occupants were armed was not a good idea.

Fortunately, two men stood leaning casually against the walls of their cubicles in a discussion. One wore khakis and a collared shirt. Efficient, business casual. The other wore faded jeans and a wrinkled knit shirt that fit snugly against a well-developed chest. Comfortable, good old boy. The name plate on the cubicle next to him said Czerwinski.

I waited with a polite, friendly smile for them to look my way. Finally, the one leaning against the Czerwinski cubicle eyed me with a measured look of physical comparison. His satisfied smirk and primitive grunt told me he claimed a personal victory.

"Need something?"

"Looking for detective Thornton. He around?"

Czerwinski nodded towards a nearby cubicle.

"Hey, Thornton. You got a live one."

I maintained a friendly smile. My gut told me Czerwinski was rude and disrespectful as a general rule. Or he might have a thing for zombies. Best not to explore it. People can be surprisingly layered and Czerwinski was a guy I didn't want to unpeel.

An African-American man popped up and approached. He was early 30's, clean cut, and wore a tailored shirt, tie, and sport coat.

"Can I help you?" he asked.

I handed him an introductory letter from Glenn Howard. Glenn had a good working relationship with all the law enforcement agencies and said it would help pave the way for me. He was right. Thornton extended his hand.

"Mark Thornton," he said.

"Jack Sterling," I replied taking it.

"A little over qualified for this work."

I shrugged.

"Beats working fast food."

Now curious, the other two wandered over. Czerwinski snatched the letter from Thornton and read it.

"You know, Czerwinski, you could have just asked to see it," Mark said.

Czerwinski snorted and read on. He looked up and appraised me carefully.

"SEAL, huh? I thought SEALs ate nails for breakfast. Don't look that tough to me."

"Yeah, but I can blow things up and hold my breath under water a really long time."

Czerwinski handed the letter to the other guy who looked it over, handed it back to me and extended his hand.

"Bob Sanderson. If Glenn Howard says you're okay, then you're okay."

I smiled and shook his hand. Almost unanimous acceptance. Czerwinski was the hold out. A guy that loved you or hated you and made his decision on the spot.

"So you leave the world's most elite fighting force to round up 2-bit criminals."

I almost said my real ambition was to become a 2-bit detective, but decided it wouldn't build rapport.

"Glenn says you're all stand-up guys and I should check in. So here I am…and looking for leads on Jimmie Parker."

Czerwinski snorted.

"A punk."

"A Gulf War vet that served two tours," I said. "Might rate a grade higher than punk."

Czerwinski snorted again. Apparently his most accomplished form of communication.

"Seeing that he shows up for his impending court date."

"But he's disappeared," said Thornton.

"Poof. And his bail has been revoked. Checked his mom's address. She gave me a phone number that led to an apartment. But no Jimmie. Checked around the neighborhood…no leads. Checked public records…no leads. So now I'm grope—uh, grasping."

"Apartment is where I apprehended him," said Thornton.

"So he's not going back there," I said stating the obvious.

"Has a sister in Lebanon, but an obvious next place to check so I doubt he'd go there either. Nothing else to offer, but you can check back with me."

He handed me a card with his cell phone number.

"Appreciate it. By the way, I'm curious about a tough, wide body kid named Jerome who hangs down by Maple Street."

"Jerome Smith. Was a promising linebacker at Dunbar High School. Now a drop out and gang member. Small time right now, but an up and comer if he doesn't get knocked off first. Why?"

"He and two buddies were the neighborhood reception committee."

"Then watch your back," said Mark. "Jerome will gleefully insert a lethal object in it."

"But no worries," said Czerwinski. "Thornton has Jerome's number. Right, Thornton? Takes one brother from the hood to take down another one?"

Thornton smiled at Czerwinski. A pleasant, unreadable mask perfected over a lifetime of deflecting comments by jerks.

"And lucky for me I have a vacuously, intelligent white man like you to school me."

Czerwinski maintained a smug, superior smile. Completely missing the jab since it was doubtful he understood the meaning or would take the time to look up the definition of vacuous.

Mark nodded at me.

"Give me a call if you need anything else."

I thanked him and left.

Glad it was his case and not Czerwinski's. I'd be totally on my own. And twice as lost.

~ELEVEN~

"Who's Paxco LLC?"

"What?" Gary Chalmers replied.

Gothic Girl was absent from the receptionist desk at Chalmers Realty when I arrived so I walked straight back to Gary's desk and found him staring intently at his computer screen. He looked at me and blinked like waking from a dream. The fear in his eyes said it was probably a nightmare.

"Paxco LLC," I repeated slowly with emphasis. "Name of the company listed as owner of all the homes recently sold on Maple Street."

"Oh, that," he said with a dismissive wave. "Investment property for the client. I don't deal with any of the principals. All handled through an attorney. Now if you don't mind, I have work to do."

He was lying. Sleazy and untrustworthy. Take advantage of nice, little old ladies without a tug of conscience. And I just plain didn't like him. Stella was right. Something bogus about a guy that colors his hair to hide his age. But there's no law about being sleazy or protecting the interests of clients.

"Who's the attorney?"

"You're the detective, you tell me."

"Never said I was a detective."

Apparently word travelled fast around here. Or maybe people in Dayton lacked enough other things to do.

"I...I have an appointment and I'd like you to leave."

I smiled pleasantly, but didn't budge.

"I mean it. Or I'll...I'll call the police."

He reached for a landline phone, but I snatched it away and leaned towards him, still smiling.

"Sure. You've been very helpful. Have a nice day."

I shoved the phone into his chest. Not painfully hard. Just enough force to make a point. Then I left, went to the parking lot, climbed into Flash and waited. I should be working to find Jimmie. Instead, I decided to squeeze Chalmers and see what happened.

In a little while he came out, got in his car and pulled out of the parking lot. I followed closely to be obvious. To make sure he saw me. To make him sweat. He drove to a nice home in Centerville with a "For Sale" sign in the yard where he met a couple driving an expensive looking SUV. I parked across the street and waited. Then followed him to another home where he met another couple. Afterwards, we drove back to his office where he hurried inside and I parked, got out and leaned against Flash. He peeked out several times. Hoping, I'm sure, I'd get tired and leave. But I didn't. Just kept leaning against Flash and grinning at his storefront.

Finally, a black, double axle pickup truck with a tool box behind the cab and mud flaps with a picture of Yosemite Sam firing two pistols and the words "Back Off" pulled in beside me.

Two burly guys in jeans and dirty white t-shirts got out and sauntered over. Both were tanned and one wore a cap with "Cat" printed on it. Both also had large, hairy forearms and generous mounds of stomach. Tough and strong, but probably slow and in poor physical condition.

I stayed against Flash going for a look of casual nonchalant. A muscle car right about now would greatly enhance the effect. But you work with what you have and Flash was it.

Cap man had a tough guy look on his face. I think he was going for frightening, but it came out more like a squint in the glare of sunlight.

"What are you doing, Buddy?"

"Working on my shopping list."

"Except you been working on it for two hours," the other man said with a smirk. "You must be a slow writer."

"Slow writer, fast reader. And how would you know I've been here two hours? You just pulled in."

"Never mind, we know lots of stuff and it's time for you to get lost."

"Wow. That's it exactly. How did you know…I'm in the middle of an existential crisis?"

"Huh?"

"That in contemplating the bane of my existence I've suddenly realized I'm not who I thought I was…and need to find my true self."

"We're talking about get lost as in take off," said cap man. "To keep your existence."

The two men laughed and exchanged a high five. They could be funny too.

"Well then. Can you tell me about the origins of galactic noise, the molecular composition of star dust and the symbiotic relationship between vacillating nosselators?"

"You trying to be smart?"

"Always trying, seldom successful. But perhaps I can draw from the astute perception and knowledge of your two great minds."

"Look, Buddy. You're not wanted around here, so why don't you just get in your little girlie car and leave?"

Honestly, that one hurt, but I didn't let it show. I could be tough too.

"Why would a grocery store not want me around?"

"Cause you ain't shopping, that's why."

He grinned, pleased with his joke. Now on a roll and already formulating an entire monologue. But I didn't think he was funny at all. Probably in the delivery.

"Okay. Let's go shopping. But I get to push the cart."

"Well, we asked nicely. So now it's time for persuasion."

"Wow, persuasion. That's a pretty big word. You practice saying that in your big, manly truck on the way here?"

There was no misunderstanding of the mocking tone in my voice. It was an open challenge. One these guys understood and would physically respond to. Not sure why I issued it. Wasn't my nature to back down from fights, but didn't usually invite them either. And yet, here I was inviting a fight. Wanting it.

If I was in to psychoanalysis, I'd probably objectively surmise the reason was because I was currently dealing with multiple, stress factors creating internal emotional turmoil. And all those emotional pressures boiling within were mounting for a volcanic eruption. Except I wasn't in to psychoanalysis. Or care to examine my personal motives, which at the moment were clouded by an unexplained, rising anger. I just knew I was ready for a good old fashioned brawl.

Cap man reached for my arm, which I snatched away so he missed. But he had committed himself fully to the grab, his weight moving forward and caught himself against Flash. I stepped aside, around and pivoted to face him. Effectively, switching positions. He was against the car and I stood where he had been.

He came at me again, but rather than move away, I stepped forward and kneed him in the groin. There was a sudden, surprised look on his face followed by a howl of intense pain and he collapsed to the ground, curled into a fetal position and moaned.

I turned to face the other guy who telegraphed his move with a big, wide swing that I ducked easily. He followed with a second that I blocked, then countered with two jabs to the nose and a combination to the stomach. As he doubled over, I stepped in, planted my leg behind him and shoved so he fell back to the pavement in a sitting position, his legs spread in a V. Blood poured from his nose and he gasped for breath.

A small crowd from the grocery store collected to watch, so I decided it best to leave. Gary Chalmers watched from inside his front, plate glass window. I smiled and waved at him, got in Flash and drove away. Suave…debonair…driving a domestic, compact car.

That evening I heated a microwaveable dish of lasagna and watched a home improvement show where a handyman renovated an old house. It was inspiring to watch something useless and worn out transformed into something new and relevant. If only that could be true for people. Maybe even with me. Although today, I felt like I had accomplished something worthwhile. Just no idea what it was.

~TWELVE~

I checked Mom's address in my phone as I approached her duplex. It looked the way I remembered. Although all the duplexes in this community of duplexes looked the same. But there was a difference today from my last visit.

Lying casually on the little porch of her front door was a large, intimidating looking black Lab. Was this her dog, or was the dog confused by so many identical duplexes? With all the changes going on in Mom's life, a dog for companionship made sense. At least the address checked out.

This one gazed at me with intelligent brown eyes that were neither friendly nor hostile. Perhaps, curious? He wasn't tied up so that as a good sign. And while I didn't exactly trust a strange dog, I did trust Mom. Couldn't imagine her with anything that wasn't friendly or at least non-threatening. So I gave him the benefit of the doubt.

"Hello there big guy, how are you?"

I cautiously held my hand out as a tentative offering, which he carefully sniffed before allowing a light pat on the head and soft scratching behind the ears. He nuzzled for more as I passed him, knocked on the door and stuck my head inside.

"Mom?"

"C'mon in Sweetheart. We're in the kitchen."

I heard other voices and wondered who the "we" was. Don't remember Mom being all that social. But then, maybe that was because of Dad, not Mom.

The Lab followed me inside demanding more attention. He licked my hand for more petting, even to the point of standing, putting his paws on me and almost knocking me over with his strength, which was significant.

"Whoa, okay, okay. I want to be your friend too. But take it easy will you? Man, with friends like you, who needs enemies?"

We continued our exchange, his playful enthusiasm increasing and my petting, scratching and rubbing around his ears, neck and stomach. We moved from the entrance foyer and down the hall towards the small kitchen in the back where the voices came from.

"Hey, Mom, " I said laughing as the Lab and I entered the kitchen, "When'd you get the—"

I stopped. Sitting at the kitchen table was Mom, four cute little girls and Beth—all dressed to the hilt. The table was set with nice china, a delicate tea set and a basket of muffins. A carefully orchestrated, all girls event.

I was dressed in old shorts and a tattered Ohio State Buckeyes t-shirt. Ready to engage in manly work helping Mom unpack and put her house together. Except the entire home appeared in perfect order. Like Mom had lived here for years rather than a week. Wasn't sure what I expected, but it certainly wasn't high tea at noon.

It was an awkward moment. A pregnant pause. And painfully obvious to everyone that I was the outsider. Only the Lab seemed undaunted. He continued jumping on me and then hurried over to Beth, seeking her attention as if to say, look what I found? What do you think, can I keep him? Mom broke the silence.

"Jack, what a delightful surprise. We're having tea. Would you like to join us?"

The four girls giggled and I grinned. That would take awkward to the extreme. Mom wore an elegant red dress with hair done and make-up like she was entertaining VIP's. I'd forgotten how attractive she was and right now she looked years younger. A rare moment where I was speechless.

"I uh...I uh...just thought you might need help putting things away. Mom, you look great!" I finally blurted and immediately felt really stupid.

"Sorry, I didn't mean to interrupt. Uh...when'd you get the dog?"

Mom smiled and nodded at Beth.

"He belongs to Beth. I think you two met on my move in day."

Beth rose and extended her hand with a dazzling smile that was genuine and unpretentious.

"Perhaps with all the work during the move, not officially. It's great to meet you, Jack."

I was speechless again. Twice in less than 5 minutes. Had to be record. Sleek looking in a gray pants suit, Beth could easily model any fashion magazine. Tall—I guessed something over 5' 9"—with a slender, athletic build that was also, gracefully feminine. Dark, brunette hair with a healthy shine and thick body that brushed her shoulders. Penetrating blue eyes that radiated warmth and intelligence. And a genuine, compelling presence that said she was more than a pretty face. And her grip was firm and assured.

"These are girls from my daycare center and Ruth is graciously hosting our tea party."

She stroked the head of the black Lab.

"And this is Sammy."

"Jack was just honorably discharged from the Navy and has moved to Dayton," Mom explained to Beth.

Sammy excitedly ran back and forth between Beth and me, licking our hands enthusiastically and demanding we both pet him…which we did.

"Sammy, settle down!" Beth commanded. "I don't know what's gotten into him. He's usually more reserved around new people."

"My animal magnetism," I said. "Or maybe something I stepped in outside."

I made a big show of removing each shoe and carefully sniffing each one.

The four girls at the table—all scrubbed, shiny and cute as a bug's ear—giggled.

"Hmmm. Not the shoes. Must be the animal magnetism."

They giggled harder.

"Are you Miss Beth's boyfriend?" one asked and they all giggled again.

"Not that lucky," I replied and immediately felt my face flush. All I knew for sure was Beth didn't have a ring on her finger, which meant nothing.

"You can be my boyfriend," the girl said. "I think you're cute."

"Well, that would be an honor," I replied and bowed.

Beth took it all in stride.

"Now ladies," she reprimanded playfully, "genuine relationships are not simply about dashing young men who captivate women with their animal magnetism. Regardless of their...uh...attractive odor. Genuine relationships are developed over time. Even in faith, your relationship with the Lord is something you have to pursue."

"And I'm all about pursuit right now…especially when surrounded by so much beauty," I said.

Again I flushed. First I was speechless. Now I was sticking my foot in my mouth. Two for two in both. Might be good to talk less.

"Jack is a private investigator and is tracking down a dangerous criminal," Mom explained.

The eyes of all the girls widened with even more admiration. To them, I probably looked just like a flamboyant, private eye on TV. Or at least, one could hope.

"Except they're only dangerous when you actually find them," I said. "And since I'm not having much luck at that right now, we're all safe."

"But you will," Mom said.

I smiled and nodded with a confidence I didn't feel.

"I know nothing about investigating, but people are connected through relationships," said Beth. "Find those and you'll find people. That's where I would focus."

"Yes, well my work is done here. I'm sure there's a fair maiden to rescue…a sweet, little old lady that needs help crossing the street...a cat stuck in a tree."

I kissed Mom on the cheek.

"Check on you later. And..."

I smiled at the girls and avoided looking at Beth.

"It was a pleasure meeting all you beautiful young ladies."

"Wait," Mom said.

She handed me a book.

"This is really good. Promise me you'll read it."

I glanced at the title. Something about a carpenter.

Not sure why a book on home improvement, but was sure she had a reason.

"Okay, Mom."

Sammy followed me to the door, romping playfully as if to say, "No, you have to stay."

On one hand, I wanted to stay and on the other, I was relieved to go. And no one was even shooting at me.

~THIRTEEN~

I returned to Jimmie's neighborhood to see if I could find someone...anyone with useful information about him.

A lady walking her dog in the neighborhood called him "A nice man who fixed her clogged sink." The man in the apartment over Jimmie was a security guard who I woke up, which soured his already sour disposition. He worked third shift and slept days so he didn't know any of his neighbors. Several other people said they knew Jimmie only by sight. I wondered why he bothered to leave. Seemed like the perfect place to hide.

I was leaving Jimmie's unit when a young lady wearing a bookbag, carrying a bag of groceries and herding three young children approached. I held the outside door open for her and waited to see which apartment she went to. She stopped in front of the door across the hall from Jimmie's apartment.

"Pardon me, ma'am. I'm trying to get in touch with Jimmie. Do you by any chance have his cell phone number?"

"Sorry," she said. "I really don't know him that well. Actually, just to say hi."

"Yeah. Seems to be the neighborhood standard."

She was petite with blondish hair falling mid-neck. Probably late 20's or early 30's and attractive. But tired looking, like she'd already seen too much hard life. Still, there was a determination about her.

She had keys in her hand and tried to insert them into the door, but couldn't manage with the bag of groceries in her arms.

"Here, let me help."

I took the groceries so she could unlock the door and push the kids ahead of her inside. I held the door open with my foot and handed her back the groceries.

"Thanks," she said.

She carried the bag over to a kitchen table, put it down and started putting things away. I continued holding the door open with my foot, knowing not to enter uninvited, but hoping my good deed might obligate her to a little more conversation. Now, what to talk about?

I noticed a pile of textbooks and class notes spread out on the table. Quick deduction. Mom was in school pursuing a degree. Bettering her life and the life of her kids. Explained the determined spirit I sensed in her. Maybe I was getting the hang of this detective thing after all.

The three kids all began engaging in different activities. Like following a familiar routine.

A curly, dark haired boy around 8 turned on the flat screen TV and a video game. The girl, a dirty blonde around 5, engaged with a smart phone. And the youngest, a towhead boy around 3, picked up a toy fire truck and drove it around the living room floor. Along with complimentary engine and squealing tires as he navigated sharp turns. There was something familiar about it, but don't know why. Couldn't remember any scene like it from my own childhood. I pushed it aside. Might not have any other opportunities like this and needed to keep the woman talking.

"Your husband working?"

"Haven't had one for several years," she replied.

She swept her hands in the air to indicate the apartment.

"Might not look great, but it's better."

I nodded.

"The phone number I had for Jimmie is disconnected. Tried to find him at home. You see him lately?"

"Been gone all day. And you've probably noticed people around here keep to themselves."

"Hard to miss."

She smiled ruefully with a nod. I noticed the title "Anatomy and Physiology" on one of the textbooks. Tired and beaten down, but not defeated.

"So you're in school."

A question in the form of a statement. The book was a dead giveaway. And I, the astute investigator, pieced it together.

"Halfway through a nursing degree. Plus I work and along with these three…"

I gave her my best "I know what you mean" look of empathy. Although clueless on what life was like for her. But my mission was unchanged. Keep her talking. Maybe she'd give me something. Anything.

I nodded at the refrigerator—a bulletin board of information. There was a calendar, selection of business cards and variety of scribbled notes all held in place by merchant magnets. Pizza delivery, medical care and one for Digger's Pub.

"I'm Jack."

"Sherry," she replied.

She hadn't made a move back towards the door and I hadn't made a move inside. A stalemate I used as permission to keep talking.

"Digger's Pub a local hot spot?"

"Wouldn't know. But the food's good. I order take out and they deliver."

Keep the conversation going, Jack.

I noticed what looked like a recent family picture on the wall of her and the three kids. And an older picture on a lamp table—a younger version of herself in a cheerleader outfit.

"Happier times?"

"A brief, smiling pose doesn't always mean happy. But you take what you can get."

I nodded at the books.

"But you have a goal and a plan. Maybe the final chapter hasn't been written."

She shrugged.

"I'm hoping."

"Hope is powerful. Seen it make a big difference in a lot of ways."

The curly black-haired boy quit the video game, poured out a pile of plastic attachment building blocks from a plastic container and began latching them together in a construction project. The girl switched on the TV to a children's program and accidentally knocked over the boy's blocks. He retaliated by hitting her, she hit back and an all-out fight broke out. Mom pulled them apart and plopped them on either end of the couch with a stern look.

"Lizzy, Matthew, five minutes time out for both of you!"

Matthew was close to the towhead. He kicked the fire truck out of his hand across the floor and the younger boy started crying. Sherry picked him up and hugged him, glaring at his brother.

"Okay, now you got 10 minutes. Want more?"

Matthew settled into the chair with crossed arms and a surly pout as Sherry looked at me with a sigh.

"Sorry I'm not much help. But I have to make dinner and drop the kids off at childcare so I can go to class."

She cleared her schoolwork from the kitchen table along with some kind of portable, medical unit about the same size of the text books. Then addressed the sister and the brother in turn.

"You can get up. You stay put."

She looked back at me.

"Jimmie seems like a nice person. I hope he's okay."

"I'm sure he is," I said. "Thanks for your time."

I pulled the door closed and heard the deadbolt slide into place as I left.

Sherry seemed genuine. And I admired her resolve. I'd never met her before today, but couldn't shake that familiar feeling. Another life, maybe? Didn't really believe in one, but no harm keeping an open mind. Disbelief in a supernatural didn't mean there wasn't one. And I had no concrete proof in either direction. I'd certainly seen enough unexplainable things to make me wonder.

And something else. Sherry was lying. Couldn't put my finger on how or why I knew, but was certain of it. How did I learn the truth and would it make a difference? Because people lied for lots of reasons. And self-protection was a big one for a single mom.

I checked the mail boxes by the entrance on my way out. The name on the box of her apartment number was Burton.

I sat in Flash and typed notes into my phone from the conversation and everything I had observed. Not sure what if anything was relevant, but you never know.

As I drove away a brown, full-size American made sedan with dark tinted windows followed me home and parked on the side of the street opposite my garage apartment. A vintage look, but it was clean and shiny with wide, sparkling white wall tires. An unusual feature these days. Not subtle about following me either so whoever it was wanted me to know or didn't care. I could follow others and others could follow me. But why?

Maybe for intimidation. Seemed to be a thing for all my recent encounters. Or maybe a power kick. I know you, but you don't know me, which puts me in the driver's seat. Faceless enemies are unnerving. Understood that as a navy SEAL since we invented the idea with our legendary, cloak of night, special ops. Never knew when or where we would strike and no safe haven was ever completely safe.

I knew all this so refused to be easily intimidated. I walked outside and headed directly toward the back of the car to get to get the license number. Perhaps a little brazenly reckless. Maybe my own manhood was at stake?

What if it was Jerome out to exact revenge? He could easily roll down the window and play target practice with an assault rifle. Had I insulted his manhood enough for that level of retribution? I'd heard of gang members killing people for less.

Too late for that now. I was already in the street. Easy pickings if it was Jerome with an assault rifle.

My only defense was to dodge behind the car out of the line of fire.

But as I maneuvered towards the back of the car, it started up and pulled away before I could see the license number. Score one for him. He was still the faceless enemy, which gave him an advantage. Score one for me because my bravado and life were intact. Or did that count for two? And which one did I value the most?

He made his statement and I made mine. Did it mean anything in the grand scheme of life? Another debate for agents of the cosmos I suppose. But I was now officially a real private detective because I just encountered my first mystery.

~FOURTEEN~

Beth's words stuck with me. *People are connected through relationships. Find those and you'll find people.* It was good advice. People don't live in complete isolation. Jimmie had human relationships at some trackable level. Find them. Follow them and they would lead me to him. Piece of cake.

Beth's penetrating blue eyes stuck with me too. Did I detect in them an interest in me or my own wishful thinking? For the moment, it didn't matter. Had no time or money for any relational pursuit but Jimmie. And Mom. Still couldn't figure that one out. Whatever was going on with her was clearly for the good. Never remember seeing her so happy. So content. Full of…joy?

I wanted to support it. But didn't understand what "it" was. A mystery within a mystery. And I was clearly awkward around all those who had it. So how do you support something you don't understand and puts you awkwardly around people that make you squirm?

I started canvassing the area around Jimmie's apartment again. Third time's the charm. If nothing else, I should get points for persistence. Maybe Carlos the bail bondsman would pay me for trying hard? Definitely wishful thinking.

Cheng's laundry mat had cleaned some of his clothes. Phil's barbershop cut his hair. Phil was your typical chatty barber and Jimmie not a chatty customer, but tipped well. Jimmie's quiet, thoughtful nature was consistent. Not sure his tipping habits were relevant. But I typed it all into my notes.

Clerk in the gas station/market store said he often bought incidentals like milk, bread and toiletries. Everyone agreed when you talked to him, you did most of the talking. The more I learned, the more it didn't add up. Jimmie wasn't the kind of guy that robbed a store at gun point. What changed?

I was finding connections, but none that were helpful. And it made me wonder. Can a person exist with human connections but no meaningful relationships? Seemed that way in Jimmie's case. So far, no one I'd encountered admitted knowing Jimmie well enough to provide any useful information. "Admitted" being the operative word. Some of them were lying. But to talk to as many people as I had so far and learn absolutely nothing had to set some kind of record for failure. Pretty discouraging too. So like any other well-adjusted person looking for encouragement, I stopped by Diggers for a drink. It was the closest thing to stability I'd seen in this otherwise transient neighborhood.

Digger wasn't there. Instead, the bar was tended by a pimple faced kid wearing a Dayton Flyers shirt. Had to be at least 21 to serve drinks, but he looked barely a teenager. Acne will do that to you. He was also rail thin, hair stuck in disarray like a fresh morning wake and hadn't yet run a comb through it.

Due to an ultra-thin neck, his Adam's apple popped out like a huge knot that jumped up and down when he spoke. Put a hula skirt on it, have him sing a two-octave song and it'd be an entertaining show. He was chatty and eager to talk. Naturally outgoing or just professionally friendly? Hard to say. The generously seeded, prominently displayed tip jar might be a slight giveaway.

That along with the fact that I was seated at the bar for less than 5 minutes with a drink and already knew his name was Richie, he was a junior at the University of Dayton majoring in economics, minoring in sociology and worked as a bartender with the goal of minimizing his already massive student loan debt.

On cue, I obligingly slipped a bill into the tip jar and took Jimmie's listening approach to see how it panned out. Richie made it easy.

He asked where I worked to which I simply replied "contractor" and took a long drink.

A word that could mean a lot of things and solicit follow-up questions, but fully satisfied Richie's curiosity. And easily diverted him when I tossed the question back.

"How about you? Worked here long?"

"Since the beginning of the fall semester. Hours are flexible, tips good."

He nodded at the tip jar and winked at me. I smiled back, touched my right index finger to my forehead and saluted him. A silent message of mutual understanding.

Roger that. Know exactly what you mean, Kid.

Establish rapport. Keep him talking. Maybe he'd say something useful. Maybe not. Even though I didn't relate to him in the slightest. Two could play the same game.

"How are classes going this semester?"

He shrugged.

"The usual. Tons of reading and homework. Several papers to write."

He held his hands up to present the room.

"Although this is all fodder for my sociology papers."

"Yeah? And what about your mudder?"

He looked confused. Either Richie was not as astute as he thought or I wasn't as funny as I thought. I opted for his astuteness. My ego was a bit fragile right now.

"So what have you learned about the human condition working at Diggers?"

Richie assumed a pose of scholarly introspection. A pseudo-intellectual who never missed a meal, but was fully qualified and prepared to articulate his expert opinion. As expert as it gets when living off your parent's high-limit credit card.

"It's interesting how the causality and science of human behavior and philosophical reasoning intersect."

"You know the same can be said about the educational similarities of college and pre-school."

He raised his eyebrows in genuine curiosity. A teachable moment.

"How so?"

"By merging the teachings of Socrates, Aristotle and play-dough."

He smiled. Processing the information for meaning, but the confusion in his eyes said he fell short. I think he did, at least, realize I was joking. Because he tried to relate to his customer. Since the customer is always right…at least up to where he stuffs money in the tip jar.

"Isn't life funny? Sometimes philosophy fits like a shoe into sociology and other times sociology fits like a shoe into philosophy. You need a shoe horn to separate them."

He laughed like it was the funniest joke ever. And I joined him. But I was laughing at the hilarity of him thinking he was funny.

"Yes, and I wonder when people who live in the Artic get together for socials…do they start off with icebreakers?"

Richie laughed even harder. Couldn't tell if he actually got it this time or was faking it.

"Probably depends on the idiosyncratic nature of the group," he replied.

Lesson. When all else fails, use big words. It'll make you sound smart.

"What I can tell you is there's an endless cycle of poverty and drug use around here."

Had already observed that, but time to play along. Keep Richie talking. See if it led to anything useful.

"Caused by?"

"Lack of education."

I popped a handful of peanuts in my mouth and washed them down with a drink.

"If people know more they'll achieve more?"

"Education opens the door to opportunity."

"And lacking that opportunity locks them into the cycle?"

"Generational poverty. When one generation is handicapped by a low ceiling of education it's difficult for the next generation to surpass it."

Sounded like a textbook quote, but I gave Richie the benefit of the doubt that it was original. I was low on cash and hoped affirmation worked instead.

"Meaning you don't know what you don't know."

He looked at me quizzically. As if surprised anyone from this bar could match his intellect. So I added.

"Maybe it's less about knowledge and more about hope."

"Support your position."

He was on an academic idealism roll.

"To gain hope you have to experience it. And that's hard when you've been beaten down by hopelessness your whole life."

"You've been to college."

It was half question, half declaration. I shrugged a yes.

"While in the Navy. Uncle Sam's nickel so why not?"

"You see action?"

"Some. And I heard a guy named Jimmie who lives around here is a vet too. Has a construction business and maybe I should look him up."

"Yeah, he and Digger are tight. Share war stories all the time.

I stared hard into my drink. I'd just uncovered a real lead and didn't want Richie see the excitement in my eyes.

"Did Jimmie take classes at U.D. too?

"No, the University of Cincinnati, I think. And I guess an undergraduate degree in psychology doesn't qualify you for a corporate executive position, but surely, something better than a handyman."

Not sure why, but I took a wild shot.

"There's a young lady that lives in the neighborhood that I think comes in. Sherry Burton. Know her?"

"Yeah. Comes in for carryout."

"You don't deliver?"

He shook his head.

"Although I'm sure franchise is the next rung on the ladder."

"She know Jimmie?"

He shrugged.

"Seen them talking. Not sure it means anything one way or the other."

"She resembles a girl I went to high school with. Know her maiden name by chance?"

"No, sorry."

"So, Jimmie goes from human repair to home repair. Go figure, huh?"

"Yeah. Life's a mystery."

He winked and moved down the bar to another customer. I smiled back and saluted with two fingers. Two fingers signifying we were intellectually, like-minded compatriots. Three fingers indicate male bonding and I didn't want to go that far on only one bar date.

So Sherry lied about Digger's food delivery and both Sherry and Digger lied about how well they knew Jimmie. There was a connection between the three that Sherry and Digger were downplaying—

obviously covering for Jimmie. Even if it was a close friendship, didn't mean they knew where he was, but they might. And if they knew, how did I get that information from them?

As I left the bar and walked to Flash parked on the street in front of Digger's, I saw the full-sized, brown sedan across the street. No hesitation this time. I boldly crossed the street to get the license number, but it started up and quickly sped away. Missed again.

~FIFTEEN~

I returned to the Montgomery County Courthouse to see if I could dig up any new information. The property owner of the address of Digger's Pub was Robert Smith. No telling where the name Digger came from. Apparently, he was still paying it off because Main Street Savings and Loan held a lien on the property.

Robert Smith had one civil lawsuit filed against him. A customer in Digger's Pub was injured in a fight and sued the other guy and the bar. But the case was dismissed because multiple witnesses testified the plaintiff, who was drunk at the time, was the one who started the fight.

But I came up empty for Sherry Burton. Probably because I had her married name and really needed her maiden name. But how did I get it?

Then a brainstorm. I searched social media sites on my phone and found Sherry Burton as Sherry Miller Burton. Picture and everything. Including the name of her alma mater, Stebbins High School. And pictures of her and her kids. Also found a business page for Jimmie with pictures of remodeling jobs and his disconnected phone number.

I searched the name Sherry Miller and learned she married and divorced Gary Crider. The divorce transcript accused Gary of adultery. And listed one child—Elizabeth.

A few years later there was a marriage application for Sherry Miller Crider and Ron Burton. Sherry listed an address in Dayton and Ron in Cincinnati. She worked as a waitress and he was a truck driver. Found no divorce record so maybe she was still legally married to Ron, but separated. Or she and Ron lived in Cincinnati when the divorce took place and where I'd find the public record. Not that it mattered. Just curious.

Felt like I was suddenly on a roll so I went by the library and looked up Paxco LLC in the business directory. It was listed as a financial investment holding company and gave only the name of an attorney—James Lawson—as a contact. Verified what Chalmers told me except now I had the attorney's name. Not that it did me any good. If the idea behind a holding company is to hide the identities of its owners, Lawson wouldn't tell me just because I walked in and asked. Even if I asked nicely.

Now had some things to consider so I stopped at home, ate a sandwich and walked along Fifth Street thinking about the case. Trying to piece together what I had learned so far. Wasn't much.

Jimmie was educated, but worked as a one man home improvement business. He listened more than talked. Sounded like a guy who was caring and compassionate. And a war vet who understood duty and honor. Course, some vets struggled with PTSD, so might need to figure that into the equation. I had discovered some relationships, but still, nothing significant enough to leverage.

Bottom line? Knocking over a drug store just didn't make sense. But he had. No denying it. And I didn't understand why his reason for the crime mattered to me. But it did.

I passed by a church with a sign on the outside that said Fifth Street Community Church and heard music from inside. The church building was old looking. Like a city of Dayton original. With traditional, religious architecture—pillars, arches and stain glass. But the music had a modern sound and captivating quality to it. The contrast between sight and sound made me pause and I sat on the front steps and listened.

I heard acoustic guitars, a box drum keeping the beat and a clear, young female voice singing with male harmony.

There is a fountain filled with blood drawn from Emmanuel's veins. And sinners plunged beneath that flood lose all their guilty stains. Lose all their guilty stains, lose all their guilty stains. And sinners plunged beneath that flood lose all their guilty stains.

The sound acoustically reverberated from within the ancient building. An old melody...an old message...in a modern arrangement. Was anything about it relevant for today? If not, why did people hold on to it so dearly?

My total religious experience was that one Easter service as a kid. I faintly remembered the preacher mentioning God's unconditional love. But having never returned, I had no context or any other perspective on what that actually meant. Just a vague sense that God was perhaps a benevolent being that loved and embraced you regardless of what you did. Which made no sense in my view of justice.

My military father had drilled into me individual responsibility and accountability. And the consequences of bad choices. So I couldn't accept a benevolent love with no sense of justice. Where did that leave psychopaths who massacred thousands, even millions of innocent people? It's okay, don't worry about it, I love you anyway? Didn't work for me.

Over the years I picked up clips of sermons by TV and radio evangelists while channel flipping. And heard a few inspirational messages by military chaplains representing multiple faiths in one sermon. But those messages were usually so theologically watered down with political correctness they were feel good, inspirational thoughts at best. And generally left me more confused.

Everyone had a different take. In fact, with all the world religions, philosophies and wacko's out there, along with multiple versions within Christianity itself, I couldn't decipher a common theme. Was God a benevolent, milk toast nice guy or a sadistic bully counting up all my wrong doings so he could torture me in hell for eternity? I couldn't make any of it work so I quit trying. I'd follow my own path and take my chances with eternity...if there was one.

The sun was going down when I stood to walk home. Inside the church, the voices launched into another song.

At the cross, at the cross where I first saw the light and the burden of my heart rolled away. It was there by faith I received my sight and now I am happy all the day.

There were times of happiness in my life for sure. But all the day? Sounded like wishful thinking. But one could still hope. Speaking of which, I had a new hopeful thread to pull.

~SIXTEEN~

That night my dream replayed a SEAL team mission. We were in Mosul, Iraq where there was heavy fighting between coalition forces and insurgents. Insurgents captured and held an American missionary couple for ransom. They demanded an exchange for insurgent captives held by coalition forces or threatened to behead the missionaries.

Our rescue mission used stealth, the cover of darkness in the dead of night and the element of surprise. Hit hard and fast with precision.

Intelligence sources confirmed the location and as we breached the front door, we entered a sparse living room with a couch, two easy chairs and a coffee table. The couch and chairs were occupied by three men with AK 47 rifles. Unfortunately for them it was pitch black and they sluggishly woke from a deep sleep. Too sluggish.

We had night vision goggles and laser targeting assault rifles with suppressors that sounded like a cough when fired. Only a few coughs and all was silent. Using hand signals, we quietly made sure the first floor was clear.

I motioned towards stairs leading up to the second floor. Could be more insurgents up there.

But the two voices—male and female—that began singing softly from one of the rooms upstairs told us probably not.

> *When peace like a river attendeth my way*
> *When sorrow like sea billows roll*
> *Whatever my lot that has caused me to say*
> *It is well, it is well with my soul.*

We found the couple tied up in a room and as we whisked them away, I was amazed by the look on their faces. I had expected fear and dread. The terror of an impending, horrible death. Instead, they radiated peace and serenity. And a month later they were right back where they had been, doing the same thing prior to their capture.

It baffled me. Why risk their lives again?

Knew the answer for myself. I was a soldier defending my country. To the death if necessary. But I faced the prospect with grim acceptance. Couldn't say I had complete peace or serenity about it. I was uncertain about what came next. Simply chose not to think about it.

I was driven by a mission. Confront and overcome the enemy by force. Not hate exactly, although I despised them for sure. Cowards who used women and children as shields and randomly slaughtered innocents. Perpetrating terror, pain, hardship and death rather than peace and prosperity. Make life worse rather than better. Senseless, twisted thinking that was perfectly right in their minds and perfectly confusing to mine.

And yet the missionaries responded in love. Perhaps a little twisted too? Certainly not rational to me. Sure, I'd heard the "love your enemies" teaching. But had never seen it demonstrated like this. Radical love versus radical hate. Could one really overcome the other? Or were they simply opposite emotions that forever pressed against each other?

It was hard to process. Ideology grows from personal convictions driven by a sense of truth. But what truth? Where does it come from? And how does it form within you? Or is there more than one truth? You have your truth, I have mine and they're different. And that's okay. But then, which one of us is right? Or we're both right? Or no one's right?

And if there is no one truth or a right truth that everyone agrees on, maybe truth itself is merely an illusion. Or at least, for all practical purposes, doesn't matter. Only power and who controls it so their version of truth prevails. Based on my observation of how the world actually works, maybe it was the most relevant explanation.

The last thing I remembered in the dream was a voice. Resonate, unfamiliar and puzzling. But clear.

You're not the only one who made a sacrifice. I sacrificed too. And it's your path to new life.

~SEVENTEEN~

I rose at six in the morning, ran three miles out on the bike path along the Great Miami River clocking 5:30 a mile, then turned and ran back. I showered, shaved, downed a cup of instant coffee, microwaved and ate a bowl of oats and headed south on interstate I-75 towards the University of Cincinnati.

U.C. was an oasis of academia plopped in the middle of urban blight showcasing ghetto living in every direction off campus. As a city, Cincinnati's roots went back to the 1800's and some of the buildings looked like original construction. Although sprinkled in, signs of trendy, urban renewal weaved a patchwork of old and restored buildings.

The Registrar's office confirmed that Jimmie graduated a year and half ago. And I stopped by the psychology department to see if anyone remembered him. A young woman at the reception desk typed on a laptop with an open textbook and cell phone in reach.

She typed on the keyboard for a while, paused to read from the textbook, then picked up the phone to text. Type, read, text. Type, read, text. Had a certain rhythm to it. I waited for her to notice me, but apparently she had a three at once, multi-task limit so I cleared my throat to get her attention.

She looked at me and immediately, self-consciously checked her hair. It was unstyled, straight brown and hung mid-neck.

"Can I help you?"

Her serious brown eyes had the naïve look of an underclassman. So I took on the persona of a suave, debonair private detective and handed her my I.D. with a smile that radiated confidence. It produced the desired effect.

"Wow, are you really a private investigator?"

I smiled and nodded humbly.

"Hoping you can help me with a case."

"Really? I mean, I'm just a part-time administrative assistant."

"Oh, come on...uh..."

"Stacy," she finished.

"Stacy," I said. "You're obviously a grad student."

She beamed.

"Sophomore. But I've carried extra hours every semester and will be a second semester junior in the fall."

I nodded encouragingly. Her academic superiority was obvious.

"And I bet you know every psych major in the program."

"Most of the upperclassmen. Underclassman are so immature."

"Look like you're twenty-one, act like you're two."

"I know, right?"

"Arrested psychological development."

She rolled her eyes.

"Especially the guys."

"The emotional behavior of preadolescent boys in the bodies of men."

"Exactly."

I held up a picture of Jimmie.

"What about Jimmie Parker. Remember him? He was here a year and half ago."

"Oh, sure. He was the exception. Of course he was a grad student. And a veteran who was a little older than most of us. Had the biggest crush on him. But I was a freshman and don't think he ever noticed me."

"We miss a lot when measuring people by external measures rather than depth of character and beauty of spirit, don't you think?"

Pretty sure it was a line I picked up from a public television children's program. She blushed and fixed her hair.

"I know, right?"

My obvious understanding of the human condition and the inequality of academic, social stratification encouraged her to open up.

"Jimmie had a natural gift for counseling. A way of listening. Made you pour your heart out to him."

"And after he graduated?

"Think he landed an internship in the behavioral unit at the University of Cincinnati Medical Center. But don't know after that."

"Do you have his last address when he was a student?"

"I think so, but I'm not sure I should give that out. Is he in trouble? I mean, what's this about?"

"It's about $40,000 and I need to find him soon or that money is forfeited."

It wasn't a lie. Just not the exact truth.

"Guess it won't hurt to give out his last address. I doubt he's there anymore."

She made a few clicks on the computer, scribbled on a piece of paper and handed it to me.

I smiled and gave her a thumbs up.

"Stacy, you're awesome. And good luck with the rest of your schooling."

"I hope you get that money to him," she said.

"We'll see."

~EIGHTEEN~

I was buzzed into the psych ward at the U.C. Medical Center. Said I was there to visit Mr. Smith. A long shot that actually worked. Maybe luck was turning my way?

Inside was an open, common area arranged to resemble a modern living room. Furnished with discount quality, couches and chairs. Fake wood floor in the form of tiled squares with an area rug. Just like home. Except the lingering odor of antiseptic cleaner and the door in and out was securely locked.

A flat screen TV mounted in an overhead corner blared away a game show. And people scattered around the room were engaged in various activities. Some watched TV, others texted on cell phones, a threesome played cards at a table. Calm and order.

Outwardly looked like ordinary, human behavior, but lacked genuine, relational interaction. Like something staged. Or people closed within themselves. Made the environment feel off. Like it was too orderly, too normal.

Of course I didn't hang out at psych wards much and ignorant of normal for the abnormal. Maybe this was it. No one looked or acted obviously crazy. But in my view? Only a crazy person would be here willingly.

To the left was an administrative office with a heavy, sliding glass window—a potential refuge in an emotional crisis. Individual patient rooms attached to the perimeter of the common room.

The nurse in charge looked all business. Crisp, white uniform, dark hair, and precisely applied make-up. The name plate on her desk said Elaine Foster. Slightly older than me and attractive. Although contained, like the controlled presence in a potentially out of control environment.

"I don't see Mr. Smith in the common area, so he might be in his room," she said.

"Honestly, I'm here for another reason."

"Oh?"

Shields up full.

I smiled my highest charm wattage to no effect. Her demeanor screamed by the book. Definitely not a Stacy. So I displayed my investigator license and took a direct approach.

"I'm looking for Jimmie Parker. He was arrested for armed robbery in Dayton and freed on bond, but has disappeared with an impending court date. I understand he was an intern here."

Elaine smiled without warmth. A professional response for appropriate moments. Carefully separating her personal and professional life. Was she married? Have kids? Believe Elvis was alive?

"Yes, James worked here. But that is a human resources issue. And of course, you know personnel records are highly confidential."

If she wasn't married, why not? Maybe too much emersion into the world of psychological dysfunction hampered her own relational health?

Okay, too much speculation. I needed to focus and get out of here. Place was giving me the heebie-jeebies.

"Understood. I also know you're in the business of helping people. And right now, Jimmie needs help."

"Armed robbery just doesn't sound like James."

A gleam of humanity peeked through her countenance.

"Never does. And if I don't find him and get him to that court date, his troubles multiply. I'm not here to dig up his past or invade his privacy. Just looking for anything to help me find him. He's a vet, I'm a vet. We don't leave a man behind."

No lies or shading the truth this time. But real empathy. Real emotion. And a touch of patriotism for extra weight. Jimmie was a brother who was broken and lost. Someone I really wanted to help.

Elaine's steely blue eyes examined me hard. And I felt exposed and a prickly sensation. Like a frog, painlessly dead, being carefully dissected. Then she picked up her phone and dialed.

"Doctor Snyder, there is a private investigator seeking information on James Parker—a former employee. You should handle this."

Doctor Snyder was Elaine Foster's alter ego. Warm, personable and completely disorganized. Late 30's dressed in business casual. Not big, but trim and fit. Intelligent, but not overly intellectual.

Case files and papers were scatter over his desk. Several professional certificates in frames were mounted on the walls. A book case stocked with volumes of Freud, Jung, and Skinner professionally supported the psychological environment.

There were also pictures of himself and family—an attractive wife and two kids. Along with a few soccer trophies. He had merged his professional and personal life into an eclectic display. He pushed a gym bag off the couch to clear a sitting space for me.

"Lunch workout," he explained.

"Operant conditioning?"

He smiled in appreciation.

"More like obsessive, compulsive behavior. But when you deal with mental issues all day, you have to decompress. Slightly more complex than B.F. Skinner's stimulus, response and positive reinforcement theories."

"But there are positive benefits to exercise that reinforce the behavior," I said.

He shrugged.

"Feel better. Function better. Try to minimize the analysis paralysis."

"Sometimes a cigar is just a cigar."

He smiled.

"I haven't met many private investigators, so I guess I have a stereotype in mind."

"Feel the same about shrinks."

"And your conclusion?"

I shrugged.

"None at this point. Life's a mystery. Still trying to solve it."

"And what have you uncovered so far?"

"Most answers only lead to more questions. How about you?"

"There are intersections between psychology and spirituality. Elements of belief, faith and hope in each. I bounce among them never sure when and where I've gone from one to the other."

"And what do you believe?"

He looked thoughtful. It wasn't the first time he'd considered it.

"A higher power, for sure. Everything about this world suggests intelligence. But what form? There's so much chaos…evil…pain. If there's a God, I don't think he cares much."

"Did his thing and checked out?"

He shrugged.

"That's the crazy thing about beliefs. They often make no sense. There should be some kind of universal standard, don't you think?"

"I think crazy is an ironic word choice."

"Yeah. Me too."

He shifted into professional mode, pulled a file from a cabinet and opened it on his desk.

"There are strict laws governing the release of personnel records," he said.

"We're just two guys talking. I'm not out to hurt Jimmie. But he's in trouble and only making it worse by running."

Doctor Snyder gazed at me speculatively, made a decision then looked through the file.

"He was hired as an intern. Generally a career stepping stone. And had a knack for counseling that went beyond the normal. Even with some of our most chronic patients, Jimmie gained incredible results. I really expected him to have an extraordinary career."

"But he leaves, moves to Dayton and starts working in home construction? Does that make sense?"

Dr. Snyder sighed and ran a hand through his thick curly hair and smiled ruefully.

"Lots of burnout and turn over in this industry. Especially for people with passion and strong ideals."

"Because there's a lot of personal, emotional investment in the work," I finished.

His sad smile and nod acknowledged my observation.

"You've counseled?"

"Surmised."

"Well, you're right. And maybe the flip side to Jimmie's problem. His empathy crossed the line of healthy boundaries between patient and therapist. And he was a glutton for punishment. Along with his work here, he counseled at a halfway house and women's shelter."

"Remember the names?"

"Sorry, no written record. Just remember him mentioning it. You have to maintain some distance for the sake of your own sanity…"

He nodded at the family picture on his desk.

"And those you love."

"And what kind of family did Jimmie have?"

"Know he regularly visited his mom in Dayton. But didn't talk about it much. Mostly a loner, which is bad in this business. You can only absorb so much and then you need emotional and psychological release. And I suspect, he may have carried some baggage from the war. But he kept it contained. May have expressed itself in other ways, though."

"Like?"

"Random headaches, chronic fatigue, dizziness."

"Was he treated for any of that?"

"Don't think so, but not sure. Sometimes called in sick because of it. Wish I was more helpful."

I stood and shook his hand.

"You talked to me. I consider that helpful and appreciate it."

He handed me a card with his cell phone number.

"Call if you have other questions. I don't think one mistake defines a person. Jimmie is a good person. I hope you find him."

"Me too."

~NINETEEN~

I drove through the neighborhood of the address Stacy gave me and decided canvassing it would be a waste of time. To call it transient was an understatement. Looked like residents probably changed every semester and Jimmie had been gone over a year.

Instead, I went to the Hamilton County Court House in downtown Cincinnati and checked public records for Jimmie. Marriage, property, liens and mortgages. Even civil and criminal records. Zip. The guy was completely clean up to now in Dayton and Cincinnati. So what changed?

I also checked under Burton and discovered Ron and Sherry's divorce records. According to the transcripts, another child was involved and the records indicated alcohol and abuse. So Sherry had been married twice and had a child with each husband. Confirmed what she told me. She had a knack for picking losers and her life now, though struggling as a single mom, was better.

As I left Cincinnati I called Dr. Snyder on his cell.

"You ever have a patient named Sherry Burton?"

"Hang on."

I heard him type on a keyboard.

"No. We had a Ron Burton. Alcohol rehab. Is this related to Jimmie?"

"Possibly. Not sure. Do people in rehab get many visitors?"

"Yes and no. Don't know this guy and there isn't any helpful information in his notes. Sorry."

"That's okay. Just following leads. Not sure it's even relevant."

I hung up. Another puzzle piece. Another thread. Not sure if it meant anything or led anywhere, but I'd keep pulling. Maybe something would unravel.

~TWENTY~

I took a detour through the city of Lebanon located northeast of Cincinnati and southeast of Dayton. An Internet search showed two auto salvage yards and I found Jimmie's sister, Carol at the second one.

She lived in a turn of the century, two-story farmhouse next to the salvage yard. An 8-foot high, chain-link fence with privacy screen surrounded the property to discreetly hide its contents.

A boy and girl around six and seven took turns pushing each other on a tire swing hanging from the branch of a large oak tree that completely shaded the front yard. Carol sat in a wicker chair on a wide, covered front porch holding a glass of lemonade and smoking a cigarette. There was a glass pitcher sitting on a small table next to her. She looked late 30's, slightly plump, dressed in jeans, a denim shirt and cowboy boots. I half expected to see an old western saloon next door.

The kids gave me only a glance but Carol sipped from her glass and watched me thoughtfully as I approached.

"Don't look like a cop or salesman. But something with Jimmie. Repo?"

"In a way. Fetching him for an impending court date."

"Bounty hunter."

"Bail enforcement sounds so much nicer."

"Don't have that ornery look. Give you that."

"Former military. Same brotherhood."

"But still taking him in."

"Sometimes you help a fallen comrade by walking with him through the pain."

Carol nodded, took a drag and breathed it out as she poured a glass of lemonade and handed it to me. I sat in the other chair and we both gazed speculatively at the kids playing on the swing. The lemonade was cold, sweet and refreshing.

"Gulf War changed Jimmie," she said.

"War does that."

"He devoted himself to helping others, but no one helped him."

"Not too late."

"Don't know where he is. Wouldn't say if I did. Even though I like you."

"I'll take what I can."

"Jimmie liked fixing things. Was always taking things apart and putting them back together as a kid. Liked fixing people too. But it took a lot out of him. Maybe too much."

"So he went back to fixing things."

"He was a perfectionist and wanted things done right."

"In construction that's called craftsmanship."

"Why he worked for himself. Tried working for another company, but they cut too many corners. All about profit, so he quit."

"What company?"

"Waggoner construction. Big outfit in Dayton."

"He also counseled at a women's shelter in Cincinnati. Know the name?" I asked.

"The Lighthouse. Appropriate for him. He was like a light for those in darkness."

"When he himself was lost."

"Don't make much sense, but there you go."

We sipped on lemonade in a moment of comfortable silence. Letting our thoughts gather and process. Watching children play on a tire swing. Silently acknowledging a hardship of life we would never completely understand.

"Maybe not lead the way, but point toward the path," I concluded.

"Yeah," she agreed. "That."

~TWENTY-ONE~

Waggoner Construction headquarters was a modern office building edifice in the Kettering area. Large, lavish and commanding. From its slick, glass exterior that gleamed effervescent in the sun to its plush greenery in a huge atrium and indoor fountain. A statement of wealth and influential community presence.

I smiled radiantly at the attractive brunette at the reception center in the middle of what could best be described as a jungle paradise. I half expected to see and hear tropical birds.

"May I help you?" she asked.

"Yes..."

I paused dramatically...since timing is everything...to heighten the tension for delivering my line.

"Is this where I register for the next safari?"

To my utter amazement, she didn't crack a smile. Didn't even blink. But her quick response humbled me in the presence of comeback greatness.

"I'm sorry. Amateur comedy night try-outs are on Mondays. I suggest you come back then and...bring more original material."

"Oh...I was...uh...well...uh, actually here to see Eric Waggoner."

She handed me a business card.

"Here's his cell phone. He's out on a construction project."

"Thanks...I...uh..."

Searched desperately for a comeback and had nothing.

"Appreciate it."

"Certainly."

She smiled. Not genuine. But business friendly and with a sense of victory.

"And FYI. Whatever your agenda, Eric does not have a sense of humor."

I called Eric when I reached the car and told him what I was doing. He invited me to visit him at a commercial construction project—the renovation of a large grocery store. I found him in the job site, mobile trailer office.

He was early 30's around 5' 10' and fit. He wore fashion statement work jeans, work boots and a stylish knit shirt with a prominent brand logo. The look of a regular guy with upper class distinction. His handshake was firm and commanding. A guy that's busy and important, but always makes time for the little people. The fact I was taller, more fit and also in command didn't appear to faze him.

"Heard about Jimmie's legal problems. Surprised me. Doesn't sound like him at all."

"Join the consensus. How long did he work here?"

"Months. Need to see records to say exactly. Had a great work ethic. But struggled with our proprietary construction methods."

"Sister says he's a stickler for quality."

"Correct. And quality is important. But so is profit. Has to be balance."

"And Jimmie thought yours skewed too far towards profit?"

He shrugged.

"Difference of opinion and perspective. From his perspective, his main concern was producing quality work. And that's good. My perspective includes other considerations. I'm concerned with quality work, meeting payroll and keeping the company in the black."

"Looks of your headquarters says you're comfortably in the black."

"Looks and presence are important to the business. Image and reality are sometimes closely aligned and other times completely independent."

"Which one are you?"

He smiled.

"Depending on the season, both. How much trouble is Jimmie in?"

"Armed robbery is significant trouble. And jumping bail doesn't help. Trying to find him."

"Can't tell you much. Jimmie was passionate in his work, but private. Didn't say much about himself."

"I've heard."

"Give you what I can. I'll have Rhonda prepare a file for you. Leaving out confidential info, of course."

"Of course."

"She'll call you when it's ready."

"Is Rhonda the brunette that works the reception center?"

"Yes, why?"

"Great sense of humor."

"Oh? Didn't know that."

"Yeah, well, thanks for the time."

We shook hands firmly and his grip out firmed me.

"Call if you have any other questions. I have no hard feelings for Jimmie and really wish him the best."

"Will do."

I left and headed towards Flash bemoaning another dead end. Then saw something that stopped me short. I turned, headed back to the trailer and poked my head inside. Eric was talking to a construction worker.

"Sorry, one last question."

"Sure."

"Do you know a real estate agent named Gary Chalmers?"

Eric shrugged.

"Sure. He's a real estate agent. I'm a builder. Our paths cross, but we're not close or anything. Is he somehow involved with Jimmie?"

"No, another case I'm working on. Just wondered. Thanks."

Eric smiled.

"Dayton is not that big. There's a lot of networking. I'm sure you have your network, too.

I smiled back.

"Of course."

Just didn't tell him my main contact was an 11-year old girl.

As I pulled out the gravel road of the work site, I noticed the brown sedan with dark windows sitting across the street around 30 yards down the street. But this time, I was ready. I pulled out a pair of binoculars, focused on the front license plate and typed the number into my phone.

As I drove away I contemplated my conversation with Eric Waggoner. Learned nothing new from what he said about Jimmie. But did make a new discovery. Because parked in the makeshift, construction parking was a black, double axle pick-up truck with a picture of Yosemite Sam and the words "Back Off" on the mud flaps.

~TWENTY-TWO~

In every private investigator TV show I ever watched, the private investigator always had real cop friends. And now I knew why. Real cops have access to important tools that private investigators don't...the National Crime Information Center and the Bureau of Motor Vehicle records.

Now that I finally had the license plate of the brown sedan following me, I needed to tap into those databases. And I knew who to ask. So in keeping with stereotypical, crime solving protocol, I stopped at Centerville Donut Shop, a local landmark, to pick up an appropriate bribe.

It was an unremarkable looking, brick building on Main Street with a simple sign out front. But the constant flow of traffic through the parking lot 24/7 advertised its popularity. When I entered, the sugary smell of donuts triggered the pleasure centers of my brain causing me to salivate.

The inside was as unremarkable as the outside. Featuring well worn, vinyl tiled flooring and a plain, open room, wide, not deep. A glass case displaying an enticing selection of donuts spanned most of the room and behind it, four employees hustled to serve a never-ending line of customers.

A section of counter with individual stools to the left of the glass display accommodated a few customers. And booths seating four lined the exterior wall and extended into a small, partially closed section on the north end of the room.

I joined a long line I was glad to see moved quickly. Except I suddenly had an urge to flee. Because at the counter, selecting a variety of donuts that an employee was fitting into a wide, flat box was Beth. She was dressed in conservative business casual. Grey slacks and a white buttoned shirt that contrasted her shining, dark hair. And I had no rational explanation for it. But the thought of encountering her made me nervous and I wanted to hide.

C'mon, Sterling. Man up!

Despite my personal admonishment and military resolve to face all fears, I bent my knees and hunched my shoulders to lower myself behind the man ahead of me who, wouldn't you know it, was shorter and thinner. Maybe if I stared at the floor and avoided eye contact she wouldn't notice me. Like playing peekaboo with a child. And right now, I felt like the ripe old age of two.

She finished paying and turned to leave, which meant she would pass right by me on her way out. I scrunched harder, but knew it wasn't working and felt a rising panic. I needed a football lineman ahead of me and had a horse racing jockey instead.

I knelt to the floor and began slowly and methodically tying shoe laces. Head down...face so close to my shoe I could smell the leather...intense concentration.

Take your time, Sterling. Slowly...carefully. Cross the laces, wind one around the other and through the opening underneath from behind and pull both ends tight in opposite directions. Create a loop with one lace by pinching it between your thumb and fingers...

I saw her grey pants approaching from the corner of my eye.

Don't look up. Concentrate. Wrap the second lace around the looped lace, keeping your finger in the middle to maintain an opening and push it through from the front while forming it into a second loop. Now pull both sides to tighten the knot between both loops. That's it. Wow! Perfect bow tie. Let's just stay down here a minute and admire how perfect it is.

The pants stopped right next to me.

"Jack?"

Busted!

I looked up. Then stood, hoping my face didn't look as sheepish as I felt.

"Hey, Beth. How are you?"

"Great. How's your investigation going?"

"It's…uh…progressing."

Progress is what you said when you were barely over a flunking grade. A loser just beyond total loser, which is exactly how I felt at the moment.

"I'm on my way to see a law enforcement officer and stopped to pick up an appropriate bribe. I mean…"

Yep. That did it. All doubt erased. I was a total loser. But her smile was warm and embracing.

"I so know how you feel. My daycare center is just down the street and early afternoon is when behavior gets the most challenging."

She nodded at the box of donuts she carried.

"So honestly, I simply resort to bribery. Donuts from here never fail me. Please don't think less of me."

"Not a chance," I said.

I felt my face flush. Her authenticity made her even more attractive.

"Hope things are going okay. Your mom and I have been praying for you."

"Oh, yeah. Well, still adjusting and all…uh, praying? Umm, thanks. Appreciate it."

She was not someone who made meaningless conversation. If she said it, I knew she was honestly praying for me. Whatever praying for someone actually meant. In her case, I was certain it was sincere, on my behalf and in my interest.

"Well, take care."

"Uh, yeah. You too."

She smiled and left. And I stood tall. In spite of everything, feeling better about myself. How could I not? To think Beth had a genuine interest in my welfare felt really good.

I bought six different donuts, paid and turned to leave when I heard a familiar voice.

"Hey, Jack. What's up?"

The voice belonged to Terrence. He, Warren and Jeff Loo sat in a booth with coffee, donuts and open Bibles. I walked over to them.

"Hey guys. This an over-eaters anonymous meeting?"

Terrence smiled good naturedly.

"We be feeding on the Word. Spiritual nutrition. You know, that was a really good try with the shoe tying bit."

"Brave and very warrior-like," added Jeff.

He and Terrence nudged each other and laughed.

Guess I was doubly busted. I smiled, in spite of myself. They were good-natured and simply having fun—even though at my expense. But not malicious or as a put down.

"And you guys have never done anything like that."

"All the time," said Jeff still grinning. "That's why I hang with Terrence. Makes hiding in public easy."

"Yeah, we've all been there," said Terrence. "Just enjoy calling each other out when caught. Called accountability."

Good time for me to change the subject.

"So you're feeding on the Word. Isn't there some kind of healthy, nutritional contradiction in reading the Bible in a donut shop?"

"It's not the nutrition, Man..."

Terrance threw his arms up in a sweeping move, to expressively include the room.

"It's the atmosphere!"

"And company," chimed in Jeff.

"You're welcome to join us," said Warren.

"Yeah, we could use another viewpoint," said Terrence.

"On a fact finding mission at the moment," I said. "Rain check?"

"Sure thing," said Terrence.

"But don't leave the door open unless you mean it," said Jeff. "Because Terrence will follow-up."

"And whenever you need facts, my man Warren here can hack the Internet for information like nobody's business," said Terrence.

"Hack sounds rather barbaric," said Warren. "I prefer online research."

"Yeah and he like a dog with a bone," said Jeff. "When he bites into it, there's no letting go."

Warren handed me a business card.

"I'm primarily an IT specialist that builds inter-commerce websites. But I do get around the Internet quite a bit. I am glad to help you if I can."

He looked at Terrence and Jeff with an admonishing frown.

"If you two are finished with your teasing and home spun philosophizing, can we get back to our discussion on the deity of Christ? How can Jesus be fully God and fully man at the same time?"

"Don't think we're supposed to understand it," said Terrance. "It's what you call a…uh…a…"

"Paradox," finished Jeff.

"Yeah. I mean, Jesus was a real person. He experienced everything we do. What do you think, Jack?" asked Terrence.

I knew he was trying to pull me in, to engage me in a spiritual discussion. But I wasn't going there. I gave a non-committal shrug.

"Not religious."

"But you have an opinion. A worldview. We all do."

"This is a safe place to explore scripture and ask questions," said Warren. "We're all on a spiritual journey and none of us have it all figured out."

"Okay, since you're talking about real people, I do have one question weighing on my mind," I said.

Warren smiled encouragingly, the paternal, spiritual father encouraging a toddler to take his first spiritual, baby step.

"Ask away."

"Did Jesus fart?"

Warren's smile crumpled into a look of shock at such sacrilege. Terrance was in mid-drink of coffee and blew it through his nose as he laughed. Jeff smiled, uncertain where the conversation was headed, but ready to go with the flow.

"What?"

It caught Warren completely off guard and the spiritual confidence that had marked his face dissolved into one of holy terror. It was nice watching someone else squirm for a change so I pressed forward.

"Did Jesus fart? You know, pass gas, cut the cheese, play the posterior trumpet."

Warren's face grew a deep red.

"I...I...don't see the relevance in that question."

"Terrence just said Jesus was fully God and man. And he shared all our experiences. If so, shouldn't he break wind like everyone else? And by the way, if Jesus was perfect, what would a perfect fart sound like? Or smell like? Don't give me a churchy, idealized version of God. You say he's real. I want to know how real."

"Jesus was real in every sense of the word. But this level of vulgarity is not germane to our spiritual discussion."

Warren was visibly struggling and reverting to obfuscation to cover his discomfort.

I smiled innocently and shrugged.

"Why not?"

"Wait a minute," said Terrance.

He was trying to control his laughter and wiping snot globs of coffee from the table.

"I think Jack has a legitimate point. I mean, we do talk about the humanity of Jesus, don't we?"

Warren's look of discomfort turned to horror. His friend was turning against him.

"Yes, but—"

"Well, if he's the God who created smell in the first place, I'd think he could go either way," said Jeff.

"Meaning?" asked Terrence.

"Raunchy or sweet."

"A loud blast or silent but deadly?" I added.

I was warming up to the exchange. Crass conversation was in my wheelhouse. Maybe I could get into this accountability thing after all. Terrance had another thought and almost spit out a mouthful of donuts in his haste to share it.

"Hey, maybe that's part of the story we missed in the Bible. You know, when Jesus cleared the temple?"

"A holy of holy farts," said Jeff. "Awesome in power and mighty to scatter away."

Jeff and Terrence were both now laughing so hard they were slapping the table and wiping tears from their eyes. I joined them along with people in nearby booths who had no idea what was funny, but laughed because the laughter was infectious.

Warren, however was appalled at such blasphemous talk.

"This conversation shows an incredible lack of reverence for God. It's…it's undignified."

"Maybe," said Terrance. "But if Jesus could control the smell, what does that say about election and free will?"

"And the trinity?" added Jeff. "An Omnipotent fart to the power of three might evaporate the universe."

Warren was self-righteously indignant. He closed his Bible and gathered his notes.

"This Bible Study has downgraded to obnoxious and is effectively concluded."

"Okay," said Terrance. "Then I have a parting thought."

We waited expectantly as he stood and smiled.

"Oh, man. SBD bomb!"

With no further discussion we all left.

~TWENTY-THREE~

Mark Thornton sat in his cubicle staring at his computer screen when I plopped the bag of donuts on his desk.

"This a bribe?"

"Yep."

"You think this stereotype of giving the cop a bag of donuts is going to work?"

I shrugged.

"Always does on TV."

He pulled out a cinnamon bun and took a big bite, closing his eyes to savor the taste. He took another huge bite, licked the sugar from his fingers and wiped them off on his shirt.

"So what you want, TV gumshoe?"

"Run a license plate for me?

"Wow. Going straight for a big favor. I'd at least expect a couple of ball game tickets for that. First or second row behind home plate."

"Next case," I said. "As I climb the gumshoe ladder. First case is strictly low budget."

"And I'm what, your police department inside man?"

"Every great private eye has one."

"Uh, huh. You already gone to great?"

"Thinking positive."

"So, what's the number?"

I showed him the number from my phone."

"Full-size, brown sedan with dark tinted windows. White wall tires. Immaculate condition. Been following me for some time. Like to know who it is."

"No need to run the plate. Know the car. Russell Crowe, leg breaker for Vic Falco. Falco's a bookie and loan shark that operates east side and now starting to push Opioids. Been small time till now, but expanding his presence. First Jerome, now Falco. You're pretty quick, Sterling. Attracting quite a fine group of friends."

"My compelling personality. And Russell isn't shy about announcing his presence."

"Cause intimidation is his thing. You'll understand when he gets out of the car."

I pulled a chair from the next cubicle that was empty and sat down.

"Can we talk about the Jimmie Parker case a minute?"

"You're asking a lot for a few donuts."

"You didn't actually run the plate, so technically you still owe me."

"You're the one doing the bribing. Don't get to make the rules too."

"C'mon. Let's talk a for instance."

"Talk a for instance. Is this supposed to take me from police inside man to police sidekick?"

"You can't be my sidekick."

"Relieved to know, but why not?"

"You talk too sophisticated. Like you're smarter than me."

"Who's bringing who donuts?"

He took a bite with a smug smile. Score one for him. Might as well concede and move on.

"This crime Jimmie committed doesn't make sense."

"Crimes seldom do."

He pulled up a file and scanned the computer screen.

"Says he filled a prescription at the pharmacy, walked around the store a few minutes, then pulled a gun and robbed it."

"So he fills a prescription and then robs the store? Does that make sense?"

He smiled at me with a look of mock pity.

"Got it. Crimes seldom make sense. But there has to be something more."

"What's it matter? Doesn't change anything. He did the crime, has to do the time."

"Great, so now you're quoting tag lines from old TV police crime shows?"

Mark shrugged and pulled up a video file of security camera footage. It showed Jimmie walking down an aisle of a drug store. From the angle, you could see the top of his head, but his body was blocked by shelving.

"What's he doing there?"

"Probably working up his nerve. He was about to rob the place you know."

Next the store clerk approached Jimmie in the aisle. You couldn't tell what was going on between them, but when they walked to the front counter, Jimmie held a gun on the clerk who nervously emptied the register and handed money over. Jimmie put it in his pocket and left.

Mark assumed the role of a patient teacher, pointing out step-by-step, patronizingly speaking to an intellectually challenged student.

"See, there's the gun. There's the clerk taking money from the register. There's Jimmie putting the money in his coat pocket. And there he is leaving the store. In police work, that's called armed robbery. And with this video evidence an open and shut case."

"Uh, huh. So what's under his coat?"

"What are you talking about?"

"Go back to where Jimmie's standing at the counter holding his gun on the clerk."

Mark replayed the video and I pointed to it like he had, but minus the patronizing tone of voice.

"See how he clutches his right arm tight to the side? He's holding something under his coat."

Mark looked closer, his eyes registering he saw something new, but his voice dismissed it.

"Yeah, so?"

"Why conceal something under your coat if you're robbing the store anyway?"

"Did I mention crime seldom makes sense? And in this case, stealing something else doesn't change anything."

"Might speak to his motive. That could change something."

"Maybe to his legal defense. Not to me."

He closed the file.

"Are we done here?

"I think so."

Note to self. If you're a rookie gumshoe, don't school an experienced police detective. He won't like it.

"Good. Because I'm ahead two bags of donuts and at least one ball game."

My best response at this point was humility.

"Got it. Baseball or football?"

~TWENTY-FOUR~

Vic Falco owned a pawn shop on Wayne Avenue. On the fringe, but not all the way into downtown Dayton. It had two plate glass windows with the name *Vic's Pawn Shop* stenciled on one of them. Iron bars spanned the windows on the inside and the front door that was propped open.

Vic stood behind the counter. He was short, balding, wore multiple diamond rings on his fingers, gold chains around his neck and a diamond studded ear ring. He also had a hairy chest on proud display beneath a flower festooned Hawaiian shirt that was unbuttoned nearly to the waist.

Lounging in a chair next to the entrance was a massive man of middle eastern heritage. Around 6' 8" and 300 pounds or more of hard muscle. I presumed Russell. Arms folded, legs extended and crossed. At first glance he seemed half asleep. Although the legs uncrossed as I approached the counter. And his eyes were alert, intelligent and flickered with recognition. But gave nothing else away.

Likely a gun stashed somewhere too, but only needed if someone else pulled one. Otherwise, his physical presence was intimidating enough. Hard to say if he was there to prevent thieves or just scare people in general.

Vic smiled. Warm. Welcoming. An eager, wheeler and dealer appraising his next sales conquest.

"Buying or selling?"

"Looking for information."

Vic didn't miss a beat or lose his smile.

"The library is not far. But closer to downtown. Should be open right now."

"I need something more specific."

"Specific to what?"

"To why Russell over there is following me?"

"Ah. A very direct private eye. And you're not hanging around sleazy hotels with a camera either."

"Have a photographic memory."

"It ever develop?"

"Digital imprint."

"Direct private eye with a sense of humor. How refreshing."

"New to the game. Still learning all the hidden rules."

"In that case you might want to study up. The hard knocks in this line of work can be painfully literal."

Russell grunted, but I couldn't interpret its meaning. A laugh at Vic's joke? An acknowledgement of truth? Or maybe he just passed gas. Thought I detected a grin from the corner of my eye, which could mean any of the three.

Vic and I smiled at one another. And behind those smiles we sized one another up. I was younger, bigger and much better looking. At least from my perspective. Although looks are often blindingly subjective. Vic was bigger if you counted hired help. Definitely had me in the hairy chest category. So I'm sure from his perspective, using a different set of criteria, he came out ahead.

We both had done our homework and let each other know. Cards out on the table. Two professionals—good guy and bad guy—conducting business. I of course, gave myself credit as the good guy.

"He's following you because you're looking for Jimmie and so am I."

"Because?"

"Collecting on an outstanding loan."

"The truck?"

Explained why there was no legal, financial documentation on it in Jimmie's apartment. A loan with Vic would bypass that. He continued smiling without acknowledgement and stroked the gold chain around his neck.

"Why would you think Jimmie can repay you if he's robbing a store?"

"Maybe that's why he's robbing the store?"

"Commit a crime to pay off a criminal?"

"Tsk, tsk, Mr. Wannabe Cop. You calling the kettle black? I operate a creative financial business."

"To those who can't afford your interest rates."

"To those who don't qualify with traditional lending institutions."

I shrugged. He had a point.

"So I'm doing your legwork."

His smile widened.

"Work smarter, not harder."

"Meaning you don't know where the truck is either."

"A man and his truck are hard to separate."

"And you want the money or the truck."

"Why not both? Won't need it where he's going."

"Smart and strategically enterprising."

"Yeah. Isn't free enterprise wonderful?"

"And what if I don't want Russell following me?"

"You'll have to take that up with Russell."

Russell grunted and a half-smile lit his face. This time I was pretty sure I knew what it meant.

"Even if I asked nicely?"

"Nice is nice, but it don't pay bills."

"Okay. Well thanks for your time."

"Absolutely. Nice meeting you. And you have a nice day."

"You too."

I locked eyes with Russell on the way out. His gaze and half smile had an evil glint that suggested he took sadistic enjoyment in his work. And no niceness about it. I smiled back, keeping it neutrally pleasant, and two finger saluted him as I passed.

Confident, not over confident. Professional respect, not scared. In the ring of hard knocks, be strategic about how many open cards you put on the table.

As I climbed in Flash, Russell followed and got into his brown, full-sized sedan. Trying to outrun him in Flash would be comical at best. But I had nothing to prove and no reason to lose him anyway. He was welcome to follow me all he wanted. I drove home, parked in the garage and went for a walk.

~TWENTY-FIVE~

I strolled along Fifth Street with no particular destination in mind, no particular agenda and in no particular hurry. A no particular, go-with-the-flow time of self-reflection.

My pace was under idle speed making it a challenge for Russell to follow me. But did his best to drive snail speed.

Russell the creep, doing what creeps do—creeping down the street. Judging by the sound of impatient horns and verbal abuse of people going around him it was unanimous. Everyone else considered him a creep too.

I stopped at Fifth Street Community Church and sat on the front steps, which put him in a quandary. No telling how long I would stay. There were no open parking spots along the curb on my side and he couldn't just block the middle of the street indefinitely. So he pulled a U-turn, parked on the curb across the street, got out and leaned against the car. He'd wait.

No reason to hide any more since I knew who he was. Maybe planning to follow me on foot from here and that made me smile. Russell was bigger than me, but would be no match in a foot race. Just had other things on my mind at the moment. If he wanted to spend his time watching me sit and reflect on the steps of a church then yay for him.

Music was playing from inside again. These people were serious about their music. Had to admit there was something compelling about it. Not sure if it was the melodies, the lyrics or the sincere, beautiful voices blending in harmony. Maybe all of it.

The sound was soothing. Inviting. Made me wonder what their worship services were like. Probably nothing like the Easter Service I attended as a boy. But not ready to find out. As I considered this, the door opened behind me and a guy around my age with long red hair tied in a pony tail, tattoos covering both arms and an ear ring came out and sat on the steps next to me.

"Like the music?"

I nodded.

"You're welcome to come in if you'd like. We're always open to an honest critique. Not that we don't get plenty from the congregation or anything."

I looked at him and he smiled.

"Just kidding, Dude. I'm Rusty."

We shook hands.

"Jack."

"So, Jack. You okay, man?"

"Sure," I said, even though I wasn't sure. But wasn't going to spill my guts out to a guy who looked like he was from a homeless shelter.

"You a pastor?"

I was being facetious. Rusty broke every stereotype I ever had of religious leaders.

"Actually, yes. I know, right. Don't look the part. Totally freaked out my parents when I told them I was going into ministry. But they were thrilled if it meant I wouldn't overdose in some dark alley. Which is where I was heading. What Jesus has done in my life is pretty amazing."

Wasn't sure how to take this guy. He obviously had a history. And I'm sure it included a lot of darkness and pain. But it was erased from his life.

In its place was joy and peace. And probably, if I brought up God farts, he'd laugh and engage in conversation. I was short on words. A rarity for me.

"Do you come out and sit on the steps regularly?"

"Hardly ever. But the Lord told me to come out, so I did."

"The Lord speaks to you audibly?"

Maybe he was even weirder than he looked. If that was possible. Or maybe his church was a cult or something.

"Nothing like that," said Rusty. "More like this quiet, urging. Hard to explain. But the more I grow in my relationship with Jesus Christ and respond to the movement of His Spirit, the more He speaks to me. Don't understand it myself. Just try to listen and respond."

"Can't think of one time in my life when I ever heard God speak to me."

Rusty smiled and there was understanding in it. And compassion. He'd been where I was. And I could see in him the same thing I saw in my Mom,

Terrance, Jeff, Warren and Beth. Something I wanted, but had no clue how to get.

"Jack, God speaks to you all the time. To hear him, you have to listen with your heart."

Weird. That actually sounded like something Terrance might say.

"And then what, speak to Him through my ears?"

Rusty grinned. Not at all put off by my sarcasm.

"I was going to say God already nose your thoughts, but that might be too puny. Seriously, Jack. Just be honest, man. Tell God what's holding you back. And when you're ready, submit to him. That's called Lordship."

He stood up.

"I hang out here every day. Come by some time and let's grab a cup of coffee. Or join us for worship on Sunday and you can hear the music in its final form."

I sat and reflected after Rusty went inside. Traffic moved along the street. People passed on the sidewalk. Russell waited by his car on the side of the street.

Sounds of tires on the road...footsteps on pavement...snatches of conversations. I was aware of it and yet, dull to it at the same time. Swimming in a sea of thoughts. Overwhelmed with strange emotions that made me uncomfortable. And in spite of all my self-discipline and ability to compartmentalize, I couldn't shake them. Had never been a touchy feely kind of guy and didn't like where this was going. Like I was heading toward some kind of collision. But of what? By force of will I shoved it all aside and focused my thoughts on the case.

Jimmie was clearly guilty of armed robbery. But for what reason? With all I had learned about him, it made no sense. Nor did I understand why his motive was important to me. It didn't change anything. He was guilty and had to face the consequences. If I could bring him in that is. At the moment it wasn't looking so good. And time was running out. If he wasn't in custody in time to insure he appeared for his court date there would be no bail enforcement collection fee.

Beth said to follow the connections and I had found lots of them. But couldn't string them together in a path that led in any meaningful direction.

To confuse things even more, I was suddenly encountering religion and religious people at every turn. And none of it fit the religious stereotypes in my mind so I wasn't sure what to make of it. I was intrigued and baffled at the same time.

I thought about what Rusty said and found myself talking silently to God. Or someone. Or something. Or maybe just to myself. It felt strange and awkward.

Am I losing it? I wasn't sure, but kept going anyway. I sensed that some kind of presence was actually listening.

Okay God. I'm not sure you're real. But you're real to all these people I know. I can't figure out what it is they all have. But I want it. So I'm listening.

I waited. Not sure what to expect. A voice? A bike messenger stopping to hand me note? Maybe Russell getting out of the car, falling to his knees and shouting Hallelujah! I wasn't sure. But I expected something. And got nothing.

Okay, God. Well, I gave it shot. Thanks anyway.

I stood to head home and then felt more than heard *Let it go.*

I stopped. Yep. I'm losing it. This time I spoke out loud.

"Let go of what?"

Everything. And give it to me.

Then I knew. We talked in the military about being all in. And I was when it came to a mission. But when it came to myself. My real self. I held back. It protected me from hurt, but also stopped me from experiencing something else…something rich and meaningful.

That's what Rusty had done. And Mom, Warren, Terrance, Jeff and Beth. But they had to take a chance. A step of faith. Was the risk of vulnerability worth it? I was convinced it was.

Okay, God. Not sure I totally get it. The whole thing about sin and forgiveness. Guess I've always considered myself a good person. Above average anyway. Yeah, okay, I'm no saint. And that's the point, right? You don't grade on a curve? Either you're perfect or you're doomed? And I've done more than enough to qualify for doomed. So I don't know the right words to say or what this completely means. But whatever all these other people have...that belonging...that peace and joy...I want it too. I'm tired of doing it my way and ready to do it your way. I want your forgiveness and whatever goes with it. I'm all in.

The thoughts were barely out and the response immediate. An overwhelming presence unlike anything I'd ever experienced. Surrounding me. Filling me. Mysterious but familiar. Comforting and reassuring. Washing over and through me with a sense of newness. Like a slate wiped clean. And putting something—I didn't know was missing—back in place. Didn't understand it. Couldn't explain it. But I knew. For the first time in my life...I was complete.

As I basked in whatever this was a flood of pent up emotions suddenly and unexpectedly welled up inside and released like a bursting dam. And I sat on those steps and bawled like a baby.

~TWENTY-SIX~

I walked home with light steps and a light heart. Something had changed in me. Something was radically different. Did I just undergo a mental and physiological experience? A fourth dimensional experience? Or maybe, simply a delusional experience?

Couldn't say or know for sure it wasn't temporary. But for now, the feeling was there along with this mysteriously new, personal presence. And I liked it.

Russell stayed with me too. Creeping along in his brown sedan with the white sidewall tires. The big creep. I noted the white sidewalls didn't have a speck of dirt on them. Probably scrubbed them down every night. A guy who regularly messes up people, but keeps his car and the sidewalls on his tires spotless. Now there's a human psychological study for you.

At the moment however, I didn't really care about Russell...his impeccable car or snow white sidewalls. I was on a spiritual high and thoroughly enjoying it for as long as it lasted. And wanted to tell someone. Beth immediately came to mind, but I nixed the thought.

Dude, you hardly know her. Can barely call her an acquaintance. Certainly not someone you call at random with this kind of personal news.

Hello, Beth? I know we've just met. I could be a total deviant as far as you know, but wanted to tell you about my recent, profoundly religious experience. Seriously, this has nothing to do with the fact that I think you're hot. It's all about our shared relationship with God.

Yep. That should do it. Guarantee she'd shun me forever. Besides, it was my first encounter with God. What's the expiration date for spiritual euphoria? I should give it a night and see how I felt in the morning. See if I still felt different or this was all just a momentary lapse in judgment.

For now, I forced myself to concentrate on the case. A connection. There had to be one somewhere. What was I missing?

I read through the notes on my phone. Reviewed all the facts and contemplated their meaning.

Thought about the people, mentally replaying scenes and conversations. Remembering body language and voice tones. Organizing it all in my mind was like sipping water from a fire hose.

Then of course, there was Mom, her new religious friends and my own, totally unexpected spiritual encounter. It was a lot to digest.

Wait. Something about…

I found it in my notes and called Dr. Snyder.

"Was one of the places Jimmie led group counseling called the Lighthouse?"

"Yes. I remember now because it contrasted the kind of darkness Jimmie addressed in counseling. Is it relevant?"

"Maybe, thanks."

I hung up, looked up the number, called the Lighthouse and spoke to a woman.

"Did you ever have a patient named Sherry Miller?"

"No, sorry."

"What about Sherry Burton?"

"No, again."

"Sherry Crider?"

"Yes. Do I win a prize?"

Usually I'd formulate a witty comeback, but at the moment I was mission focused. If Sherry wanted to remain anonymous, Crider was a good name to use.

The woman verified when Sherry was there, which matched the time Jimmie led group counseling. Puzzle pieces were falling into place. I called Mark Thornton.

"What prescription did Jimmie pick up at the pharmacy?"

"Albuterol."

"For what?"

"Don't know. Has no bearing on the case."

Maybe to him, but to me it was important. It spoke to why Jimmie robbed the store and I was driven to learn the answer. An Internet search revealed albuterol was a liquid medicine put in Nebulizer inhaler machines to treat asthma patients. It opened their breathing passageways during asthma attacks.

I had a product list from the drug store of all the items in the aisle where Jimmie was in the surveillance video. You could see movement and tell he was doing something, but didn't know what it was. I was convinced however, that he took something off the shelf.

Asthma nebulizer inhaler machines were on the product list. Another connection snapped into place. Sherry had two marriages and one child from each marriage. But three children.

I suddenly placed the familiar feeling I had at Sherry Burton's apartment. The boy in the picture in Jimmie's room at Mrs. Parker's house looked just like Sherry Burton's towhead son. Where I also saw a medical unit that I now recognized as an asthma treatment nebulizer machine. So Sherry and Jimmie were acquainted as more than neighbors. And Jimmie's reason for robbing the store now made sense.

What if I had a son experiencing a serious, potentially life-threatening asthma attack? And I needed albuterol and a nebulizer machine, but was short on cash?

According to the product list, the machines cost around $100.00. More cash than he probably had on hand and if the boy was in the middle of a medical emergency, Jimmie may have felt desperate. What if he didn't rob the store for the money, but to cover the fact he was stealing a nebulizer machine? So when they arrested him and recovered the money, they wouldn't know about it?

I checked my notes and called Warren.

"Do me favor?"

"Sure, what?"

"Looking for information on a Sherry Miller that attended Stebbins High School. Guessing somewhere in the late 80's, early 90's."

I heard Warren type on his computer.

"School records list an address for Sherry Miller in the Riverside area. That would be in the school district. There's a Harold and Martha still at that address."

"Any other connections?"

"Like what?"

"Like anything."

"She has an associate degree in nursing from Sinclair Community College and is currently pursuing an undergraduate degree at Wright State University."

"No help. What else?"

"Her parents are debt free. Paid off their home mortgage. Two cars—both also paid off. Carry no credit card debt. Own property out in Xenia."

"I need the address for the property in Xenia."

"I'll send it to you in a text."

"Awesome. And Warren, you're amazing."

"Really?"

"Yes. How do you do that anyway?"

"If I told you, I'd have to kill you."

He was silent and I wasn't sure how to respond.

"I'm kidding," he said. "Man, you guys tease me about being serious all the time. I make a joke and you go mute on me."

"Thanks, Warren."

"Sure."

~TWENTY-SEVEN~

I pulled out the drive and started down the street, then realized Russell was right behind me. So I parked on the curb and walked back to his car. He rolled down his window. A half-smile on his face.

"Yeah?"

Quite a talker, that Russell.

"I'd like you to stop following me now."

"Gonna stop me?"

"Hoping it doesn't come to that."

He got out of the car.

"Sorry to disappoint you."

We stood there for a moment. Both measuring the other. Then he went for his gun. But I was much quicker and was pointing mine at him before he was halfway there.

"Wouldn't if I was you."

Russell stopped. His smile tightened, but he managed to hang on to it. And now waited with a measured look. Mentally cataloguing me.

"Why don't you carefully, with your fingers, take that gun out and throw it on the ground over here."

He did. Tossing it near my feet. I picked it up. A 9mm semi-automatic. I released the cartridge and tossed the cartridge and gun into nearby waist high weeds. Then I released the cartridge from my gun and tossed them in two different directions behind me. Russell grinned with anticipation as he trotted towards me.

I was inviting Russell to fight and not sure why. Certainly didn't have to. I could have just taken his car keys, driven off and left him stranded. With this new religious thing going on I should probably take the high road. I'd heard the "turn the other cheek" Bible quote enough times to know religious people weren't supposed to look for fights. And didn't that now include me?

Instead, what I responded to was another little voice saying, "Go ahead. You can take him. Prove yourself. Teach him a lesson." And it was exactly what I intended to do.

Jogging straight at me was a little reckless on his part. Sure, he was bigger than me in every aspect, so I understood why he was confident. But he was over-confident in his approach. And that leads to mistakes. In this case, Russell not only underestimated my fighting ability, he way underestimated my vertical leap. When he was a few yards away I stepped towards him and jumped high with a front snap kick that landed, solidly right under his nose.

It rocked back his head and staggered him backwards. Would have knocked most men to the ground and possibly unconscious. But not Russell. It did, however break his nose, which now bent crooked and bled profusely.

He grunted, wiped it on his shirt sleeve and came forward again. This time, a little more cautious and in a boxer pose. His stance was good. His footwork practiced. Obviously he spent time in the ring. But he was slow. Way slow. Or maybe I was just lightning fast. Yeah, that.

He threw two punches, a right and left that I blocked easily and countered with two quick shots to the stomach which hardly phased him. I moved back and he lunged forward to bear hug me, but I feigned left, moved right, then stepped past him and pivoted around with a back-fist slam to the base of his skull. He turned to face me, rubbing the back of his head, so I know it stung, but still didn't stop him.

He advanced again, smile gone grim, angry and determined. I was perhaps, a better adversary than he estimated. Story of my life.

But I had poked a bear. Russell was not the kind of guy that beat you up a little to teach you a lesson. He was the kind of guy who beat the life out of you. And I was his intended victim. If he got me in his grasp, I was in big trouble. Maybe I was the one who was over-confident? And that mistake would not go well for me.

On the other hand, most of the people Russell probably fought weren't trained in facing sociopathic killers and I was. Maybe I was a first for him. Someone who encountered the threat of imminent death as a daily way of life. And rather than cower, engaged it.

Just in case, I looked around for possible back-up and saw none. The street was quiet. No witnesses. No one to call 911. I was on my own.

Now Russell was in full boxing mode. Moving warily. Throwing jabs. Looking for openings to close in. Fortunately, he was still slow and easy to evade. Good thing too, because if one of his jabs connected it would knock me half unconscious. But every time he threw one, he left himself open and I'd step in quickly, land a combination to his stomach, and step out.

He kept his arms up to guard against another high kick. Nose still bleeding and pausing frequently to wipe it on his shirt. But his cardio fitness was lacking. Likely, not used to fights lasting over 15 seconds. This one was already several minutes long and he was tiring...laboring for breath. And along with the bleeding nose, sweat was pouring down his face and stinging his eyes.

Finally I let him get closer and brought my right leg up for another kick. He braced for a high kick to the face, but instead, I pivoted and delivered a low side kick that connected at an angle to the inside of his left knee. It buckled with a loud pop and Russell collapsed to the ground, cradling it and grunting in pain. He tried to get up, but even through his pants leg I could see the knee swelling quickly. A torn anterior cruciate ligament.

"Sorry, Russell. You should probably have that looked at."

I picked up my gun, got into Flash and headed to Xenia. I had effectively proved my manhood, taught Russell a lesson and expected to feel good about it. But I didn't. And that was something new too.

~TWENTY-EIGHT~

The property in Xenia was in the middle of farmland. Miles of soybeans and corn fields spread in all directions as far as you could see. Farmhouses dotted the flat landscape that afforded clear visibility. So there was no sneaking up on the one I was headed for. I could see it from miles away and if Jimmie was there he could see me too.

I pulled up to an old, two-story farmhouse surrounded by a thick enclave of massive maple and oak trees that formed a shady, hedge of protection from the sun and weather.

A short, blacktop drive led up to the left side of the house and formed a parking area that spanned in front of a recessed barn. A ¾ ton pick-up with the name *Jimmie's Remodeling* on the side door was already there. I parked next to it, got out and approached the house.

The spacious, wooden front porch was newly remodeled. Complete with hanging swing. The man in faded jeans and sweat shirt with a *UC Bearcats* logo didn't even look up. He was staining the railing and was nearly finished...the last part of the job.

He nodded to a pitcher of iced tea and two glasses on a small table next to the swing. One glass was full and the other empty, but full of ice.

"Help yourself. I'm almost finished if that's okay. Hate to leave a job undone."

He was thin, but sinewy. A guy stronger than he looked. With tattoos on both arms, a receding hairline, and short cropped hair sprinkled with gray. I wasn't sure what to expect and had my gun holstered underneath my shirt. But I wouldn't need it.

I nodded, poured a glass of tea, sat on the swing and took a drink. A cool, sweet, refreshing taste in the midst of a quiet, peaceful setting. The sun was out, but the huge trees provided ample shade. Birds chirped. Squirrels scurried busily among the trees. A slight breeze carried the pungent scent of livestock. I rocked gently in the swing and simply enjoyed the moment.

"Told her this would never work, but you know women."

"Yeah."

Actually didn't have a clue on women, but wasn't going to admit it on only one glass of tea. He looked at me for the first time. Sizing me up.

"You serve?"

"Till just recent."

He nodded as if confirming in his own mind.

"Gulf War and Iraq. Naïve kid, just out of high school. Ages you fast."

I nodded.

"War is the worst ugliness of life coming at you all at once. Overwhelms a lot of guys."

"And yet, my very best friends," he said, "the ones I trust with my life, were forged in the course of war. Hard to figure."

"Yeah," I said. "Same here."

Except my life had also just taken a radical turn and was suddenly, profoundly different in a way I couldn't describe. Wouldn't make the ugliness go away. But something told me I wouldn't be overcome by it either.

Jimmie finished, put the lid on the can of stain and slid it up against the side of the house. Then stepped off the porch to admire his work.

"People ask me why I left counseling for home remodeling. Simple answer. You get to see a completely restored project. In counseling, it can take years to see even a little progress. And sometimes it's never. Weighs on you over time."

He looked at me and I could see the pain of countless lives reflected there. Some of it probably his own.

"There's just too much pain in the world and not enough hope to go around. I'm ready when you are."

I would have completely agreed with him up until just the other day. But not now. Hope is exactly what I just found. And I ended up talking about it the whole drive to the police station. Unusual for me, but like everyone said, Jimmie was a great listener and I couldn't help myself.

I started with my first Easter church experience as a kid. Fast forwarded to Mom's conversion. Meeting Terrence, Warren and Jeff Loo.

Conversations with Rusty on the steps outside his church. Left out Beth. Not sure why.

As I talked, I realized what had all seemed random coincidences now looked orchestrated. Like a master plan of carefully crafted characters and plot to affect a story outcome. And I marveled at it. I was on a new journey that excited and scared me at the same time. Because for the first time in my life, I had released control. Uncertain what it meant or where it was taking me. But strangely at ease with it.

Jimmie asked a couple of questions that kept me talking and then just listened. Another counseling session for him or were we connecting? Decided it didn't matter. I'd tell my story and let him figure out his own.

Mark Thornton was at his desk when we arrived. I introduced them and they shook hands like two guys meeting at a social event. Jimmie sat as Mark processed him in the system.

I waited for Mark to finish and shook hands with Jimmie before I left.

"Thanks," he said. "Gave me some things to think about."

"Glad to talk more if you want," I said.

"Okay," he said. "I'm anticipating lots of time. And you'll know where to find me."

~TWENTY-NINE~

Mark Thornton drove out to the farm in Xenia with me to collect Jimmie's truck. Couldn't say no since I had just gift wrapped him an arrest. He also had to endure a repeat of the story I told Jimmie, although he wasn't the same, willing listener. But I didn't care.

"It's amazing to me," I said to Mark. "Jesus was God in human form. Completely God and completely man. How does that even work? Totally baffles me. But it's amazing."

Amazing seemed to be my new word.

"Yeah, amazing," said Mark in a patronizing tone of voice. "Except the baffled part. You and baffled go well together."

"I'm serious, Thornton. God's Spirit is like…actually inside me. That's a scary thought."

"Uh, huh. Thought you were scary weird enough without God. So chill, Dude. You're not converting me."

"Yeah, okay."

Mark dropped me off and followed as I drove Jimmie's truck over to Vic Falco's pawn shop. I parked it on the street and entered the store along with Mark. Russell sat in a chair by the door with his knee propped up on another chair. He wore a knee brace and a pair of crutches leaned nearby against the wall.

I smiled like we were pals.

"Hey, Russell. Don't get up."

I tossed Vic the keys to the truck. He wore a pretend smile that did not match the chill in his eyes. Neutralizing his enforcer was not good for business.

"Here you go."

"What's this supposed to mean?"

"I just repossessed Jimmie's truck for you. Won't even charge you a finder's fee. On the house."

"Lucky me. Problem is, it still has an outstanding balance on the loan," said Vic.

"Jimmie can't pay it off where he's going."

"So it accrues interest while he's in and he can resume payments when he gets out," said Vic.

He smiled. This time real and with a sense of victory.

"The down side of taking out a financial loan."

"There's also the cost of doing business," I said. "Sometimes, you have to cut your loss and move on to something else. With the extortionary payments Jimmie has already made plus the resale of the truck, I'm pretty sure you'll make out okay."

I put a document on the counter that he picked up and looked at.

"And this?"

"Legal document saying you have received possession of the truck and you release Jimmie of any other financial claims related to it. Sign it."

"And I should do that, why?"

"Because you don't want some pesky cop in your business 24/7," said Mark. "It might, you know, discourage your other financial enterprises. Maybe cost you more in the long run."

"And why should this individual financial transaction warrant such personal, police attention?"

"Because that individual financial transaction is a real person named Jimmie. A war veteran that served his country. And that means something to me. Should mean something to you too."

"Well, officer, since you put it in such patriotic language, how could I not?"

Vic signed the document and smiled. More than forced this time. Tinged with anger.

"You two have a nice day."

Mark looked at me when we were outside.

"Have to say, that really felt good. Falco won't eat much profit, but I enjoyed watching him swallow some pride. And I assume you had something to do with Russell wearing that knee brace."

"Something."

He nodded. Didn't say it, but I might have just climbed a rung or two up the respect ladder.

"Means you're now on the enemy list of both Falco and Russell. You okay with that?"

I shrugged.

"Dealing with enemies is a way of life for me."

"Gotta say, Sterling. Might be nice to have you around after all."

"That mean I'm on your friend list?"

"Whoa. A couple donuts and one arrest? Don't get ahead of yourself."

"What if I intentionally find ways to annoy Czerwinski?"

"Definitely heading in the right direction. Just dial it back on the religion."

~THIRTY~

When I told Terrence about my faith decision, he gave me a bear hug that squeezed the wind out of me. And insisted I join his weekly meeting at Centerville Donut Shop with Jeff and Warren, which I did.

They invited me to an annual, Memorial Day picnic with some friends that Terrence hosted at his auto repair shop downtown. Terrence supplied burgers and dogs and everyone else brought drinks, side dishes and desserts.

Picnic at an auto repair shop seemed a bit odd to me, but so far, everything about my new life was different than I expected. Just hoped I didn't become all weirded out like all the religious nuts shown on the news.

I was actually a little nervous as I approached the address Terrence gave me carrying a dish of green beans. Store bought can heated up in the microwave.

There was no number in the address. Just the corner of Ludlow and Fifth Street that made sense when I arrived. Because it was an old warehouse that spanned a half-block in either direction. Consisting of massive, open space inside, a high girded ceiling with banks of windows letting in natural light and multiple garage doors along each street that were all open.

The interior was informally divided into sections. The auto garage section had seven bays and a small parking lot of cars in waiting—either completed repair and waiting for customer pick-up or waiting for repair.

Multiple gas grills with grill masters were positioned just outside the garage doors on the sidewalk cooking a steady supply of burgers and dogs. Their spiraling smoke split between the outside air and inside building where it gathered into a canopy high above at the ceiling.

The "some friends" Terrance mentioned was a huge crowd of people gathered in a designated picnic area section. Several rows of long tables were placed end to end and piled full of burgers, dogs, side dishes, desserts and drinks. Additional tables were scattered around for dining and other people brought their own folding chairs. It was unorganized, random seating, with people clustering up in family and friend groups. And being the single guy with no group who knew practically no one, I stood there a bit lost.

A third section was designated for recreation. It had two basketball courts with portable hoop systems, a volleyball court, 3 pickleball courts and 4 sets of cornhole. All full of people playing.

As I contemplated my next move, Warren appeared to rescue me. We weaved through the crowd and on the way, we passed Glenn Howard and Samantha.

"Good work on apprehending your fugitive," said Glenn. "I'll have a check by Wednesday. Stop by to pick it up and we'll talk about your next case."

Money and another case sounded really good.

"Yes, sir. Thank you, sir."

I smiled at Samantha who concentrated hard on ignoring me. She carefully squeezed ketchup and mustard from plastic bottles onto a hot dog.

"Hi, Sammy. Enjoying your day off school?"

She looked up like noticing me for the first time. Being ignored by people was becoming routine for me. Perhaps this incredible new power of invisibility would aid me as a bounty hunter.

"I guess," she said dismissively and took a careful bite of dog.

She wore jeans and a blouse, had her hair fanned out and wore make-up. The effect—which was certainly intentional—made her look several years older.

"Well you look exceptionally cute and at least 20 years old," I said as Warren and I moved on. Pretty certain I saw her blush.

Warren led me to where he, Terrence, Jeff and their families sat clustered together. I felt something brush my legs from behind and turned to have Sammy stand on his back legs and greet me by putting his paws against my chest.

"Hey, Sammy!" I said and scratched behind his ears.

He was on a leash that Beth pulled back on with little success. A handsome man, maybe a couple years older than me, stood next to her. He looked familiar, but I was sure I had never met him.

"Well I hope you're both happy," she said with a grin. "Because he just dragged me across half the building to reach you."

"Well of course," I said. "Us wild animals have to stick together."

I bent towards him and Sammy licked my mouth and nose. Then I grabbed his paws and gently lifted them off my chest so he dropped to all fours.

Beth gave me a tight hug and released me, her face slightly flushed.

"Terrence says you've committed your life to Christ. I'm so excited for you."

Her smile radiated a beauty unlike anything I had ever encountered.

"Yeah," I said.

I felt my face flush too. Tried to think of something clever to say, but came up zilch and decided best not to try. I didn't know how to describe what was going on in me, but something was definitely different.

"Oh," she said as if remembering her manners. "Jack, this is Paul Mitchell."

Paul smiled and shook my hand. He was a couple inches shorter than me, but broad shouldered and fit. Likely a former football player who still worked out regularly. His squeeze had a territorial firmness to it.

"Hear you were in the military. Thank you for your service."

"My honor," I replied.

"Jack just gave his heart to Christ," Beth said to Paul. "Isn't that exciting?"

Paul smiled with a condescending look I didn't like. I was quickly not liking the rest of him too.

"If religion works for you that's great," he said. "Personally, I've always felt people use it as a crutch."

"Yeah, used to think that too. And God just taught me something else."

"And what's that?"

"No one is as together as they want people to think. Truth is, we're all pretty broken. And the real crutch we're leaning on is foolish pride."

I smiled back.

"But that's just me."

Paul's face clouded and Beth cheerfully intervened to dispel the tension.

"Paul's family owns Mitchell's Liquidation downtown and he's running for Dayton City Council," she said. "You may have seen some of his yard signs."

I had. The yard sign across the street from Stella's house. Explained why he looked familiar. And I knew Mitchell's Liquidation was a huge, warehouse building near Dayton's minor league baseball stadium on First Street. Eight floors crammed with every item you could imagine, collected from years of liquidating businesses around the Dayton area. A giant, indoor flea market.

"Your Mom, Terrence, Warren, Jeff and I all attend the same church. Maybe I'll see you there?"

"Good possibility," I said.

My wishful imagination or did she blush again?

"Okay. Well, I look forward to seeing you there."

Was her interest all spiritual or maybe something more? I was hoping for door number two.

It took some effort for Paul to steer Beth away because Sammy fought to stay with me. Glad somebody considered me worth hanging out with.

"Forget it, Sterling. "She's way outside your league. Although if I was white, she'd be on my date list."

I turned to face Mark Thornton who wore shorts, an Eastern Kentucky University basketball jersey and cradled a basketball against his hip with his right hand.

"Dude, with you, color is a non-factor. You're like inter-racially ugly."

"Oh, yeah? Post office would be ashamed to hang your ugly mug shot on the wall."

I grabbed the basketball from him. Dribbled it around my back and through my legs.

"Want to see real beauty? Then let's take it to the court where I'll demonstrate poetry in motion."

I tossed Mark the ball and in a fluid motion, he twirled it on the index finger of his right hand. Then he pushed it into the air, caught it deftly on the back of his right hand that he lifted to meet it and let it roll smoothly down his right arm, behind his head and along his left arm where he snagged it with his left hand and tucked it against his left hip.

"Your poetry against my lightning quickness? You're on."

There was an open court that we took and Thornton started dribbling through his legs and behind his back.

"School is in session."

An enthusiastic crowd gathered to watch as we played hard, but with a sense of showmanship. Dropping three's and driving in for emphatic dunks.

He won the first game and I won the second, showing off a little with a behind the head, two-handed dunk. We decided to quit even—to protect our fragile male egos. And ended up back by Warren, Terrence, Jeff and their families with plates piled full of hamburgers, side dishes and desserts. Talking while we ate.

"Got unusual ups for a white boy," said Mark.

"Our SEAL team played a lot between missions. Most bases had a court or two. Good to help stay in shape. And learn evasive moves when bullets are flying at you."

"Thought SEALS caught bullets in their teeth."

"Only the little ones. The big ones you have to dodge."

The conversation flowed naturally going from the recent case with Jimmie to Terrence, Jeff and Warren moving in and out naturally about God and faith.

Jimmie would serve time for armed robbery. But the fact he had no priors and was acting on behalf of his son experiencing a serious asthma attack was considered mitigating circumstances. And the judge gave him the lightest sentence possible. Turned out the motive for the robbery did have an impact and I was glad to make a positive contribution to the outcome.

My first case was solved, but there was still something sketchy going on in Stella's neighborhood. Not sure what, but I would find out.

And there was this whole faith thing to figure out too. Rather than fading away, it was growing stronger and more present. More real. And an extra bonus—the chance to be around Beth, which was also a growing desire. She might be with Paul

Mitchell today, but if he didn't have this thing with Jesus, I was sure he'd never go beyond the friend zone with her.

So here I sat. With a group of people I was already calling friends. Already feeling comfortable to be around. Had enough money for the next few months and another case starting next week.

It was a sense of family I never expected outside my SEAL team. A growing sense of mission and purpose dawning like a bright, rising sun. Much still to learn and discover. But with friends beside me on a journey that was spiritual and eternal. On an adventure that was both scary and invigorating at once. And it felt like I was home.

THE END

Made in United States
North Haven, CT
02 December 2022